BOOK**SHOTS**

AVAILABLE NOW!

CROSS KILL

Along Came a Spider killer Gary Soneji died years ago. But Alex Cross swears he sees Soneji gun down his partner. Is his greatest enemy back from the grave?

ZOO 2

Humans are evolving into a savage new species that could save civilization—or end it. James Patterson's *Zoo* was just the beginning.

THE TRIAL

An accused killer will do anything to disrupt his own trial, including a courtroom shocker that Lindsay Boxer and the Women's Murder Club will never see coming.

LITTLE BLACK DRESS

Can a little black dress change everything? What begins as one woman's fantasy is about to go too far.

LET'S PLAY MAKE-BELIEVE

Christy and Marty just met, and it's love at first sight. Or is it? One of them is playing a dangerous game—and only one will survive.

CHASE

A man falls to his death in an apparent accident.…But why does he have the fingerprints of another man, who is already dead? Detective Michael Bennett is on the case.

HUNTED

Someone is luring men from the streets to play a mysterious high-stakes game. Former Special Forces officer David Shelley goes undercover to shut it down—but will he win?

$10,000,000 MARRIAGE PROPOSAL

A mysterious billboard offering $10 million to get married intrigues three single women in LA. But who is Mr. Right…and is he the perfect match for the lucky winner?

FRENCH KISS

It's hard enough to move to a new city, but now everyone French detective Luc Moncrief cares about is being killed off. Welcome to New York.

KILLER CHEF

Caleb Rooney knows how to do two things: run a food truck and solve a murder. When people suddenly start dying of food-borne illnesses, the stakes are higher than ever….

113 MINUTES

Molly Rourke's son has been murdered. Now she'll do whatever it takes to get justice. No one should underestimate a mother's love….

THE CHRISTMAS MYSTERY

Two stolen paintings disappear from a Park Avenue murder scene—French detective Luc Moncrief is in for a merry Christmas.

BLACK & BLUE

Detective Harry Blue is determined to take down the serial killer who's abducted several women, but her mission leads to a shocking revelation.

James Patterson's
BOOKSHOTS
Flames

AVAILABLE NOW!

LEARNING TO RIDE

City girl Madeline Harper never wanted to love a cowboy. But rodeo king Tanner Callen might change her mind...and win her heart.

THE McCULLAGH INN IN MAINE

Chelsea O'Kane escapes to Maine to build a new life—until she runs into Jeremy Holland, an old flame....

SACKING THE QUARTERBACK

Attorney Melissa St. James wins every case. Now, when she's up against football superstar Grayson Knight, her heart is on the line, too.

DAZZLING: THE DIAMOND TRILOGY, BOOK I

To support her artistic career, Siobhan works at the elite Stone Room in New York City...never expecting to be swept away by Derick Miller.

RADIANT: THE DIAMOND TRILOGY, BOOK II

After an explosive breakup with her billionaire boyfriend, Siobhan moves to Detroit to pursue her art. But Derick isn't ready to give her up.

BODYGUARD

Special Agent Abbie Whitmore has only one task: protect Congressman Jonathan Lassiter from a violent cartel's threats. Yet she's never had to do it while falling in love....

MICHAEL BENNETT FACES HIS TOUGHEST CASE YET....

Detective Michael Bennett is called to the scene after
a man plunges to his death outside a trendy Manhattan hotel—
but the man's fingerprints are traced to a pilot who was killed in
Iraq years ago.

Will Bennett discover the truth?

Or will he become tangled in a web of government
secrets instead?

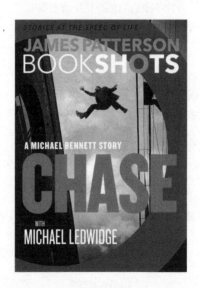

**Read the new action-packed Michael Bennett story, *Chase*,
available only from**

BOOKSHOTS

HIDDEN

A MITCHUM STORY

JAMES PATTERSON
WITH JAMES O. BORN

BOOK**SHOTS**

Little, Brown and Company

New York Boston London

Copyright © 2017 by James Patterson
Excerpt from *Cross Kill* copyright © 2016 by James Patterson

Hachette Book Group supports the right to free expression and the value of copyright. The purpose of copyright is to encourage writers and artists to produce the creative works that enrich our culture.

The scanning, uploading, and distribution of this book without permission is a theft of the author's intellectual property. If you would like permission to use material from the book (other than for review purposes), please contact permissions@hbgusa.com. Thank you for your support of the author's rights.

BookShots / Little, Brown and Company
Hachette Book Group
1290 Avenue of the Americas, New York, NY 10104
bookshots.com

First Edition: January 2017

BookShots is an imprint of Little, Brown and Company, a division of Hachette Book Group, Inc. The Little, Brown name and logo are trademarks of Hachette Book Group, Inc. The BookShots name and logo are trademarks of JBP Business, LLC.

The publisher is not responsible for websites (or their content) that are not owned by the publisher.

The Hachette Speakers Bureau provides a wide range of authors for speaking events. To find out more, go to hachettespeakersbureau.com or call (866) 376-6591.

ISBN 978-0-316-31726-9
LCCN 2016934161

10 9 8 7 6 5 4 3 2 1

LSC-C

Printed in the United States of America

HIDDEN

CHAPTER 1

MY MOODY MONGREL, Bart Simpson, kept watch from the warm backseat. He rarely found my job interesting. At least not this job.

I was next to the loading dock, folding newspapers for delivery. A surly driver named Nick dropped them off for me every morning at 5:50 sharp. What he lacked in personality he made up for in silence. I always said hello and never got an answer. Not even a "Hey, Mitchum." It was a good working relationship.

Even with the wind off the Hudson, I could crack a sweat moving the heavy bundles of papers. I used the knife I had gotten in the Navy to cut the straps holding them. My station wagon sagged under the weight of a full load. My two-day-a-week afternoon gig in Milton didn't strain the shocks nearly as bad. I usually dropped Bart off at my mom's then. My dog was as close to a grandchild as she had, and they could both complain about me.

In the early morning gloom, I caught a movement out of the corner of my eye and reacted quickly, turning with the knife still in my right hand. It was an instinct I couldn't explain. I was raised in upstate New York, not Bosnia. But I relaxed as soon as I saw

Albany Al, one of the few homeless people in Marlboro, standing near the loading dock, a dozen feet away.

The older man's whiskers spread as he grinned and rubbed his hand across his white beard. "Hello, Mitchum. They say you can never sneak up on a Navy SEAL. I guess that's true."

I was past the point of explaining to people that I was never an actual SEAL.

When I took a closer look at the old man, I realized he wasn't ready for the burst of arctic air that had descended on us. "Al, grab my extra coat from the car. It's too cold to be wandering around dressed like that."

"I couldn't."

"Go ahead. My cousin usually wears it, but she didn't show today. She's a wuss for avoiding the cold."

"I wondered where Bailey Mae was. I was hoping she had some of her coffee cake."

Then I realized the older man hadn't come to keep me company. He'd wandered over to snag some of Bailey Mae's famous coffee cake, which she handed out like business cards.

I said, "I miss her cake, too."

The old man said, "I can tell." He cackled as he rubbed his belly, but he was looking at me.

I patted my own belly and said, "It's my portable insulation." Maybe I hadn't been working out as hard as usual. A few warm days and some running would solve that.

The old man continued to cackle as he walked away with my coat.

CHAPTER 2

WHEN I'D FINISHED my route, I headed over to my office off Route 9. At least, my unofficial office. I always hit Tina's Plentiful at about 8:15, right between the early breakfast crowd and late risers. The old diner sat in an empty strip mall that hadn't been updated since 1988. A couple of framed posters of the California coast hung on the walls. No one had ever explained their significance, and none of the customers seemed to care. The place had the best Reubens and tuna melts in upstate New York, and they treated me like family. Maybe it was because one of my cousins worked in the kitchen.

The lone waitress, Mabel, named by a mean-spirited mother, lit up when I walked in. Usually I sat in the rear booth to eat and see if I had any pressing business. There was never much pressing in Marlboro. Today I headed toward the counter since there wasn't much going on and it would make it easier on Mabel.

Mabel was a town favorite for her easy smile and the way she took time to chat with everyone who came into the diner. As soon as I sat down she said, "Finally, a friendly face."

I gave her a wink and said, "Is the world not treating Miss Teenage New York well today?"

"Funny. You should cheer me up by taking me to the movies in Newburgh one night."

"Only if my cousin Bailey Mae comes with us."

"Why?"

"So you understand it's as friends and not a date."

"Am I so terrible? You've had some tough breaks and I'm a lot of fun."

I couldn't help a smile. "Of course you're not so terrible. You're also so *young*. And I'm not going to be the guy who holds you back from all the suitable young men in the area." That was as much as I wanted to say today.

Before she could answer, I glanced out the wide front window and saw my cousin Alice, Bailey Mae's mom, hustling across the street toward the diner. She is a year older than me and was only twenty when Bailey Mae was born. She is a good mom, and the rest of us help. Her usual smile was nowhere to be seen as her long brown hair flapped in the wind behind her. She yanked open the door and rushed right to me.

"Mitchum, Bailey Mae is missing."

Suddenly, the day got colder.

CHAPTER 3

I SPENT A few minutes trying to calm Alice down as we started to check some of the places Bailey Mae liked to hang out. Bailey Mae hadn't been to school that day or to the library or to the sad little arcade where she sometimes played out-of-date games. Alice had gone to sleep early the night before, after her shift at the bottling factory in Gardnertown. Bailey Mae usually came home about eight o'clock. She's a smart fourteen-year-old, and a quarter of the town is related to her.

We wandered around town, asking a few questions. No one thought it was unusual, because I am the unofficial private investigator for the whole area.

Mrs. Hoffman on Dubois Street hadn't seen Bailey Mae but took the time to thank me for finding her son, who had been on a bender in Albany and didn't have the cash to get home.

After nearly an hour, I tracked down Timmy Jones, a buddy of mine from high school who now worked for the Ulster sheriff's office.

Timmy raised his hands, showing his thick fingers, and said, "I spoke with your cousin Alice already. We're making a few checks, but Bailey Mae has wandered off before."

I knew she sometimes got frustrated and left the house, but she usually ended up at my house or my mom's house. I said, "She's a good girl."

"No one's saying she's not. But we can't just call out the troops every time a teenager is out past curfew or mad at their parents."

"Bailey Mae is more responsible. She wouldn't do something like that."

Finally Timmy said, "Okay, we'll get everyone out looking for her. But get your family involved, too. There's more of them than there are cops in the area."

CHAPTER 4

BAILEY MAE HAS always been my favorite relative, and I have plenty to choose from in Marlboro. After I rounded a few up and explained the situation, the look on my cousin Todd's face said it all: they were worried. Bailey Mae is the family's shining light. Todd is a self-centered dick, and even he was concerned enough for our little cousin that he closed his precious auto repair shop to help search.

I pulled Alice aside and hit her with some simple questions about what was going on around the house, what the last thing she said to Bailey Mae was, and whether they'd been fighting. The usual.

She said, "I told you everything. There were no problems. I haven't been drinking and she hasn't been angry. The only thing that's new is that she's been hanging out with Natty a little bit."

That caught me by surprise. I blurted out, "Natty, as in my brother, Nathaniel?"

Alice nodded. "No real reason for it. He's nice to her and she likes his car. That's all I ever hear about. You know teenagers and cars. Just another crazy dream of hers."

"Natty shouldn't be anywhere near Bailey Mae."

Alice said, "He did his time."

"He always does. But he's still a drug dealer."

"He's family."

"Maybe by New York State law, but not the way I see it."

CHAPTER 5

I PURPOSELY LEFT Alice in Marlboro when I made my way down to Newburgh. My old station wagon sputtered a couple of times but got me there in about twenty minutes. Route 9 was open this time of day and I parked directly in front of the State of Mind Tavern, just past the I-84 underpass, the dive bar where Natty, my older brother, does business. I immediately spotted his leased sports car on the side of the dingy building. Natty had gotten tired of having cars seized every time some industrious cop stopped him and found dope inside. All it took was enough weight to be charged for trafficking and the car became part of the crime—and also part of police inventory up for auction. So now he switched out cars every year. The hot little convertible was near the end of its term.

As I opened the door, the bartender looked up through the haze. They aren't as strict in upstate as they are in the city, so cigarette smoke hung in the air. The smell of toaster pizza was permanently stuck in the discolored wallpaper. The bartender, who looked like he dined on steroids every day, gave me a cursory look and deemed me unworthy of an acknowledgment.

My brother, Nathaniel, or "Natty" as he's been called his whole life, is two inches shorter than me, at six feet even, and thin as a rail from a life of drugs, coffee, and cigarettes. I had no clue why he got called Natty while I've been called by my last name, Mitchum, since childhood. Only our mom calls me by my first name.

His head jerked up instantly. Instinct from his line of work. We have the same blue eyes and prominent jawline, but not much else in common.

I headed directly toward him when the bartender, who doubled as Natty's bodyguard, stepped from behind the bar to grab my left arm. Now he wanted to dance; a second ago he was too good to speak to me. A quick twist and thumb lock with my right hand dropped the ox to one knee in pain until the man understood how stupid his idea had been. Thank you, SEAL basic training class 406.

Natty stood up quickly and said, "Tony, no need for that. This is my little brother." He moved around the table to greet me, rushing past Angel, his semi-regular girlfriend, who once posed for *Penthouse* or one of those magazines.

I held up my hand and said, "Save it."

That brought Natty up short. "Why? What's wrong? Is it Mom?"

"Where's Bailey Mae?"

"Bailey Mae? I haven't seen her in a couple of days. Why?"

"She's missing and I heard she's been hanging out around you. You're a shithead so I came here first."

"How could you suspect me of doing anything to our own cousin? I love that girl. She's got dreams."

"We all do."

Natty stepped closer and said, "Look, Mitchum, I know you don't like what I do, but it's only a little pot and I don't force anyone into anything." He put his arm around my shoulder and started to lead me back toward the front door.

I stopped short and grabbed his arm. The bartender saw his chance at some payback, stepped forward, and took a swing at my head with his ham fist. It might as well have happened in slow motion, given all my years of preparation and the months of Navy training. It was almost an insult. I bobbed back a few inches and the big man's fist passed me. Then I swung Natty into him like a bag of potatoes, and they fell back into the barstools and got hopelessly tangled together on the grimy floor.

Another guy who'd been sitting at Natty's table grabbed a pool cue and stepped forward. In an instant I had my Navy knife out of my pocket and flipped open. I needed to blow off some steam and had just now realized it. As I'd expected, the jerk focused all of his attention on the knife, so I landed a perfect front kick in his gut, knocking him off his feet. To give the guy credit, he was upright and holding the pool cue again in a flash, his face beet red from the shock of being kicked and the momentary lack of oxygen.

Natty scrambled off the floor, his hands up, and jumped between me and the guy with the pool cue. Natty yelled, "Wait,

wait!" He turned toward the other man and said, "Chuck, chill out!" He changed tone and attitude as he turned toward me. "Mitchum, just calm down and put the knife away. I want to help."

I had never heard my brother say that to anyone. Ever.

CHAPTER 6

I HAD TO fight the lunch crowd at Tina's Plentiful but somehow managed to grab my regular booth in the back. I needed to calm down and get some perspective before I even tried to get Mabel's attention. Contemplating fratricide is exhausting. At least it looked like I had one more relative in on the search. Natty had jumped in his hot convertible with his dullard girlfriend and raced back here to help our cousin Alice look for her daughter.

I needed thirty minutes to get my bearings, and the most efficient way to do it was to eat. I would need calories to help me during what could be a long day, so I gave Mabel my hand signal for one of their famous tuna melts. Her little wink let me know she understood.

The diner was busy and made a kind of relaxing noise. At least it was familiar and natural to me. After a few deep breaths, I looked up and saw an elderly woman from my route marching down the narrow space between the counter and booths, headed right for me. She lives on Robyn Drive and her name is Lois Moscowitz. I know most people's addresses and whether they get the local paper, the *New York Times,* or the *Wall Street Journal.* This one is the local-only variety. She never broke stride until she plopped down in the booth across from me.

"Hello, Mrs. Moscowitz."

"Mitchum, I need help." She had that cute, friendly local accent that made it clear she had never lived in the city.

I said, "I'm kind of booked up right now."

"But you're the only one who can help me."

"What's wrong?" I looked up at the pass-through to the kitchen and stared lovingly at my tuna melt, which had just landed.

"My husband is missing."

There were a lot of excuses I could make, but once I looked into those lonely brown eyes, all I could say was, "I'll take the case." I had to. I was the town's unofficial PI. It was part of the job description. I knew enough people were looking for Bailey Mae at the moment that I wouldn't make much difference, and this woman needed me right now.

Like a mind reader, Mabel had already wrapped my sandwich to go, tossed it across the counter to me, and blew me a kiss as I followed Mrs. Moscowitz out of the diner.

She sat straight and dignified in the passenger seat of my station wagon as Bart minded his manners and didn't try to force his way to the front. I didn't trust the little bugger enough to leave the sandwich back there, but it was good to know I had my buddy close by.

Mrs. Moscowitz didn't say a word as we drove north on Route 9 toward Milton. She didn't have to say anything; I knew where we were going.

I turned off the road and back toward a small private drive with a view of the Hudson. She glanced around but still didn't say anything as I brought the station wagon to a stop. I scurried around the front of the car to open her door. The private cemetery covered about two acres and had a lovely picket fence around the border, with a narrow, winding road that cut through the property in a seemingly random route.

The gravestone closest to the asphalt road had a simple inscription: *Herman Moscowitz. Devoted Husband.*

I stood close by in case I needed to grab her, but all Lois Moscowitz did was stare at the inscription. It could've gone either way.

Then Mrs. Moscowitz turned to me and started to laugh. Loudly. She wrapped her arms around my shoulders and gave me a hug, laughing the whole time. I needed the hug as much as she did. She was suddenly a different person. Younger, animated. As I drove her home, she chatted about her hobbies of knitting and skeet shooting and asked about my mom.

When we got to her tidy two-bedroom house, I pulled in the driveway and ran around to open the door for her again. She tried to give me a five-dollar bill and some change from her purse.

I kept refusing until she said, "How's an investigator going to stay in business if he doesn't charge people for his time?"

I finally took the cash, then waited until she was safely inside.

CHAPTER 7

I HADN'T EVEN gotten back into my car when Timmy Jones, my buddy from the sheriff's office, pulled up in his marked unit. The cold wind blew his thinning blond hair in a swirl around his wide head. The look on his face told me he had news. It didn't look like good news.

My mind raced with all the possibilities: Bailey Mae had just been found dead at the foot of a cliff, or her body had washed up on the shores of the Hudson. I'd done a good job of tamping down the darker visions of what might have happened to her. Pretty much the whole day had been spent either looking for her or avoiding thinking about what might have happened to her. That was one of the reasons I'd helped Mrs. Moscowitz. I was good at avoiding tough issues. The private investigation business was my main means of not dealing with my own emotions. If I was distracted by something else, I couldn't dwell on the past. On dead fiancées. On missed opportunities. On my screwed-up family.

My stomach did a flip-flop as Timmy slowly walked around the front of his patrol car and then up the short driveway to face me.

The frustration of his silence made me bark out, "What is it?" My voice couldn't hide the dread I felt.

Timmy started slowly, looking for the words. "My partner and I were knocking on doors, asking about Bailey Mae near her house." He paused and ran his hand through his hair.

"Timmy, get to the point," I almost snapped.

"Sorry. The old couple down the street from your cousin Alice's house, the Wilkses, were found dead inside their own house."

"Dead? From what?"

"They'd been shot."

This made my head spin. I even had to put my hand on the hood of my car to steady myself. "Shot? Bob and Francine Wilks have been shot?"

Timmy just nodded and mumbled, "In the head."

This was just too bizarre. I spoke to the elderly couple every day. If I didn't see them while I delivered the paper, I'd run into them at the diner or Luten's grocery store. Something didn't add up. All I could do was look at my friend and say, "Let's go."

CHAPTER 8

MY MIND WAS still racing as I followed Timmy, driving at his normal, conservative pace. Shit like this just doesn't happen in Marlboro. Maybe in Poughkeepsie or even Newburgh. But not here. What the hell was going on?

I was anxious to get to the crime scene but realized I needed to be with Timmy to get past any of the other cops, so I chugged along behind him. I figured I might be of some help. I'd been through a number of forensic and crime scene schools in the Navy. Since then I had been through more than a few similar classes at Dutchess Community College. I probably understood these things better than the local cops, who never had to deal with them. At least when I was a master-at-arms in the Navy, I'd seen a few crime scenes on base. And I knew the local cops' weakness: They didn't want to call in the state police unless it was absolutely necessary.

Timmy knew my background and got me past the yellow crime-scene tape and the disturbingly young patrolman who was standing guard. I got a few odd looks from the other cops, and the only detective on the scene completely ignored me as she silently made notes in the corner.

The bodies were still in place as someone from the coroner's office took photographs. They were sitting right next to each other, as if watching TV from the ancient plaid couch they probably bought in the seventies. Single gunshots, probably from a 9mm, had left holes near the center of each of their foreheads and had caused just a trickle of blood to run down each pale face. It was neat and probably quick and professional.

I glanced out the window and saw that the sun was starting to set. Where had the day gone? Then I noticed it. I moved toward the kitchen, careful not to disturb anything, and stared for a moment until Timmy eased up beside me.

He said, "What is it, Mitchum?"

I nodded toward the counter. "That's one of Bailey Mae's coffee cakes." I leaned over and touched it, then broke off a corner and popped it in my mouth. "It's fresh. She was here."

CHAPTER 9

IT WAS AFTER midnight when I finally left the Wilkses' house. The sheriff's office was still there collecting evidence and taking photographs. In fairness, I didn't have to prepare and document a criminal case. All I wanted to find out was who shot the friendly older couple and where Bailey Mae fit into all of it. That was what kept me there so long: I had been looking for other clues that pointed to where Bailey Mae was and what had happened to her.

Who says nothing ever happens in Marlboro? It had been a long, hard day.

After I snatched a few hours' sleep, I was preparing to deliver my papers early again. It gave me some normalcy and allowed me to be out in the town in case I saw something that could help.

Even Nick, the guy who dropped off the bundled papers, was interested in our sleepy little town for a change.

The husky teamster said, "I heard about your cousin. I'll keep an eye out."

I was stunned. I had been starting to think he didn't even speak English.

Then he pointed at the front page of the first paper strapped in the bundle and said, "Shame about the old couple, too. You guys need to get your shit together." Then he was gone.

He was also right. One of the reasons I stayed in Marlboro was because of the atmosphere. It is a nice place to live with nice people around. Even if I am related to a bunch of them.

By the time Bart and I were rolling in the loaded station wagon, a sleet storm had made the roads a crapshoot and visibility shitty. I had never seen the weather turn so cold and ugly this early in the year. It matched my mood about Bailey Mae's disappearance.

No one was out this morning as I cruised the streets slowly, tossing papers to some houses and walking them up to the front door at the homes of really old or infirm people. It hurt to drive past the Wilkses' house and not throw a paper. The yellow tape was still up, but the house was dark and no one was around.

Even the diner was nearly empty because of the weather as I hustled in through the driving sleet. Bart, as usual, elected to sleep in the back of the car.

I slipped onto a stool at the sparsely populated counter as Mabel walked up with a plate already in her hands.

"What's this?"

She gave me one of her dazzling smiles and said, "I knew you'd be in and knew you'd feel like scrambled eggs."

"How'd you know that?"

She just shrugged as she slid the plate in front of me. The smell was intoxicating and it really was just what I wanted.

Mabel lingered, and I could tell she was troubled by something. I didn't push it, since I noticed her checking to be sure no one was close enough to hear our conversation. She leaned on the counter and put her face close to mine. She still had that goofy look in her eyes that tends to make me uncomfortable.

She said, "Listen, Mitchum, I need to tell you something."

I didn't answer, just waited for it to come out.

"I'm worried. I've seen the same strangers here for the past few days. I didn't think it meant anything, but with Bailey Mae missing and now the Wilkses dead, I feel like I need to tell someone."

She had my attention. "I'm listening."

"Two men and a woman came in right as we opened at about 5:30 yesterday and this morning. It reminded me that I'd seen them before, a few weeks ago. They're not from around here."

"What makes them suspicious?"

"Who in their right mind would hang around this town if they didn't have to?"

"Me, for one. But tell me more about these strangers. What did they look like?"

That's when she surprised me. Instead of describing the strangers, she pulled out her phone and showed me a photograph she'd snapped of them leaving the diner. Two guys in their thirties with good builds and short hair and a tall woman about the same age who wore her dark hair in a neat braid down her back. Nothing unusual about them except they were all in good shape.

I had Mabel text me the photo, and then I gave her a stern look. She said, "What? What's wrong?"

"I don't want you risking yourself snapping photos of who-knows-what. You can tell me anything, but don't do anything stupid. Let's figure out what's going on first. Don't stick your neck out."

That was *my* job.

CHAPTER 10

I CONTINUED MY search for Bailey Mae by looking around Marlboro and the surrounding area, and I showed the photo from Mabel to the people I came across. No one seemed to recognize the three strangers from the diner.

My family had blanketed the area well. There were now flyers up on virtually every telephone pole, and most people that I visited had already talked to one of my cousins or my mother.

I decided to try a new tack and headed down to Newburgh to talk to the cops there. Newburgh was a much larger city and had seen better times. It had a crime rate that bucked the national trend by rising every year, and it was now considered one of the most dangerous small towns in the country. The city had a dingy look to it that I was afraid would never clear up.

The Newburgh cops knew me. Partly as a local and partly, unfortunately, as the brother of one of the town's drug dealers. My status as a veteran overcame some of that, but the cops still weren't thrilled with my brother's profession. Fortunately, most of the cops knew I wasn't on that level. What kind of an idiot would bust his ass on a paper route every day if he was really a drug kingpin?

The police station house was located on Route 300, not far from the State of Mind Tavern. The station was quiet when I stepped inside and walked toward a heavyset desk sergeant. I knew the big guy was from Buffalo, and I appreciated that he listened to me, paid attention, and even looked at the photo of the three strangers in Marlboro.

"I've already been keeping an eye out for your cousin and asking a few questions, but no one has seen her down here in a few days. I guess you already knew she would hang out over at the tavern with your brother sometimes."

I nodded my head, making sure I didn't add my approval to it.

A tall, muscular patrolman who had already been on the force when I'd gotten back from the service stopped to see what we were talking about. The cop was named Tharpe and I recognized him from high school. He wore his brown hair in a crew cut like he just got out of the Marines. He took a look at the photograph on my phone and said, "Sorry, dropout, don't recognize any of them." Then he turned and pushed through the swinging double doors into the control room off the lobby.

I'd heard it before. Sometimes "dropout," sometimes "washout." I got it. I didn't make it to the end of the SEAL course. It was just something I had to deal with.

A few minutes later, as I was headed out of town, I turned a few blocks out of my way to go past the State of Mind Tavern. The parking lot was packed and music pulsed from inside. There aren't a lot of nightspot options in Newburgh.

I immediately spotted Natty standing at the edge of the parking lot, speaking on his cell phone. As I pulled the station wagon to the curb, he looked up and immediately walked toward me, ending his call.

Natty said, "Hey, Mitchum." As he stepped up to the car and leaned down, he looked into the backseat.

I knew what he was looking for. I said, "Bart's at home."

"Why? Thought he went everywhere with you."

"Who can tell? Maybe he liked the warmth of the house and knew I'd be in and out of the car." When we were kids, Natty and I loved *The Simpsons*. I would pretend to be Bart and Natty played Homer. It was a blast. I have no idea when we split. Probably in high school when he found an easy way to make a buck.

Natty made a quick scan of the area, then looked back at me and said, "What brings you down here?"

"Bailey Mae." Then I held up my phone and asked, "You ever seen these three before?"

Natty studied the photograph and said, "There've been a few more strangers around lately, and maybe I saw these three around somewhere. Let me think about it some more."

As I nodded and started to pull away, my brother reached in through the window and put his hand on my shoulder. "Be careful, little brother. This isn't the Navy. There's no telling who's nuts. I'll get back on Bailey Mae's trail tomorrow. I have all of my associates out looking. We'll find her."

Maybe my brother had changed. At least that's what I kept thinking as I spent another hour stopping at a couple places on the way back to Marlboro. Bailey Mae had vanished, and she had seen the Wilkses sometime before they were murdered. That didn't leave me with a good feeling.

Once I was in Marlboro, I saw my cousin Todd and his wife out knocking on doors. It made me realize how grim things had turned in our little town. *Everyone loved Bailey Mae.* I had to stop the car at that thought and correct myself out loud. "Everyone *loves* Bailey Mae."

CHAPTER 11

IT WAS AFTER nine when I rolled up to the diner for a shot of coffee and a snack before going out again on the only case that mattered to me.

Before I even sat down, Walter, a middle-aged man from town, approached me.

He was nervous and always spoke fast. "Mitchum, Mitchum, got a second?"

I was too tired to answer. He took it as a yes. I rubbed my eyes as he blurted out, "I've got a job for you."

All I could do was stare and let him finish his thought.

"My wife is gone. Missing. I think she's in the city with her personal trainer. I can pay. Double your normal rate."

I shook my head.

"Triple."

In my head I thought, *Triple of nothing is still nothing*, but I said, "I'm sorry, I can't."

He turned and left the diner in a huff.

Now Mabel and I were alone. She actually sat in the booth with me, something she never did.

I said, "What are you still doing here?"

"Worked a double. I need money for college. I've been taking classes over at Dutchess Community College, and I just got my GED at the end of the summer."

That was one of the first things to cheer me up all day. I said, "That's great. Any idea what you want to study?"

She just shrugged her shoulders, and we stared at each other for a few seconds. Finally Mabel said, "It's not easy, is it?"

"What?"

"Life."

"Not always."

She put her chin on her hands and it made her cute face seem even younger. "You really wanted to be a SEAL, huh?"

"I dreamed about it as a kid. I practiced for it. I did it all. Ran, studied karate, pull-ups, push-ups, anything I thought would get me ready. I even became a history buff because I read that all great soldiers were students of history."

"What happened?"

"I underestimated my ability to do a basic and simple skill."

"What's that?"

"I couldn't swim well enough."

"You didn't know that before you applied?"

"I thought I just needed more practice. And I did get better, but not good enough. I was right at the top of the class, that's why they cut me a break about my swimming ability at first. Ultimately it wasn't meant to be. And I nearly drowned in the Pacific. It's deeper than you think."

Mabel laughed at that and her smile changed the whole room. It made me smile for the first time in two days.

She said, "So you could shoot and fight, but not swim."

"Basically. Now I just try to do my part in other ways."

"Like the PI stuff?"

"Sometimes."

"You don't ever feel bitter about the SEALs?"

I forced a smile. "I don't think the Navy would want that. Life's too short to waste it on regret."

She reached across and placed her hand on my forearm. "You're a good egg, Mitchum."

I put my hand over hers and said, "So are you. Now let's both go and get some rest."

I gave her a ride to the double-wide trailer that used to belong to her mother and refused an invitation inside. Right now all I needed was to lie down with Bart for a few hours and sleep as best I could.

CHAPTER 12

I WAS AS tired as I could ever remember being as I pulled the station wagon up the narrow driveway and came to a stop twenty-five feet from my front door. I liked my simple house with two bedrooms and an attic a hobbit couldn't fit in. My front porch light was on a timer and illuminated the pathway, but the inside was pitch-black. That wasn't good. I always left one light on in my kitchen. Normally, I could see it through the front window, and it cast a little light across the whole house. I didn't want Bart walking into a wall in the dark. Someone had turned it off.

The only defense I had was my Navy knife, which I dug out of my front pocket and flipped open. I use it as a tool, but its original purpose was as a weapon. The door was still locked, and I wondered if the light had just burned out. Still, I entered carefully, slightly crouched with the knife in front of me. Clouds had obscured the moon, and the inside of my house could have been a cave.

I was relieved to hear Bart's nails click along the tile as he came to me. But he whimpered slightly, something I rarely heard. I felt my way to the wall and flipped the switch that turned on the single light. Instantly my house seemed more natural. It was a light I was used to. Then I walked around and turned on several more lights, taking some time to lean down and comfort Bart. The dog was spooked. His wide little body, a cross between a boxer and a bulldog, was shaking.

The place looked in order. I checked the back door and the windows, and everything was secure. But there were a few little things out of place. The magazines on my coffee table were too straight. I wasn't that neat. They were usually plopped in an uneven pile. The drawers in my kitchen were not quite how I had left them. I remembered grabbing a pen and paper to make a grocery list and leaving my main junk drawer a mess. It was still chaos, but not the same chaos that I left it in.

My house had been searched. By professionals. Probably in the late afternoon, so they thought they were leaving everything in order when they shut down all the lights. I took a quick glance through the bedrooms and single bathroom, but nothing obvious was missing.

I immediately went to the high cabinet in my kitchen, to a stack of dish towels and extra pot holders. I stood on my toes to find the blue oven mitt I was looking for. I pulled it down, reached inside, and slid out the Beretta 9mm that fit inside the mitt like it was made for it. An old trick I learned from a chief petty officer in San Diego. No one ever wants to look through your kitchen linen.

As soon as my head hit the pillow, Bart was up on the bed,

nuzzling in close to me. I wrapped my left arm around him and kept the pistol in my right hand. I was nearly unconscious in seconds.

It felt like I had only dozed off for a minute when my alarm went off, blaring Led Zeppelin's "Dazed and Confused." Habit pushed me up out of bed, and I led Bart to the front door so he could race outside and do his business.

Bart opted to stay in the house while I headed off to work and went through the motions of delivering papers. Maybe that's why I kept this job: on the days I needed it, I didn't have to think about it at all.

I was hungry and looking forward to chatting with Mabel, so I got to the diner a few minutes earlier than usual. Now every time I walked into a public place I automatically looked for the three strangers. This morning it was just locals. But there was one surprise. Instead of Mabel behind the counter, it was the lovely Tina herself. She rarely stepped in as a waitress anymore, preferring to run the kitchen and do all the restaurant managing.

Tina had been a year ahead of me in school, and she still looked great, if a little stern. She'd always been businesslike, but this morning she acted like a Marine drill sergeant, barking orders back to my cousin in the kitchen and telling her nephew to be quicker busing the tables.

My booth was taken, so I sat at the counter directly in front of the door. Tina managed to flash me one quick smile and got right to the point. "Make it fast, Mitchum. What do you want?"

"Where's Mabel?"

"She didn't show this morning and she's not answering her damn cell."

I could tell it wasn't a good time to pursue any more questions about the tardy waitress. Not if I didn't want to risk her job.

Instead, I just said, "It's not like her. She never misses a shift. She needs the money."

But Tina's glare told me Mabel might not get a second chance.

CHAPTER 13

I MAY HAVE been overreacting, but with all the crazy shit going on around town I needed to go check on Mabel. She had seemed fine the night before. Maybe the double shift had caught up with her and she had just missed her alarm.

The double-wide trailer she had lived in with her mother, before her mother died of a brain aneurysm two years ago, was only a few blocks from the diner, at the end of a gravel drive behind the post office on Orange Street.

Every one of the fourteen trailers in the tiny park was well kept, and Mabel's had a few pieces of flair that told you a younger person lived inside. A little hand-painted street sign pointing south that said KEY WEST 2230 MILES, the doormat that read BRING JOY OR BEER INTO THIS HOUSE. I knocked on the door and got no answer. I thought about walking back to my car and grabbing my pistol. Instead, I slipped my hand into my pocket and felt my knife for security.

I tried the knob and found the door unlocked, then called out in a loud voice, "Mabel, it's Mitchum." Nothing. I eased into the front room, quickly scanning in all directions, then called out again. The heat was on, and Mabel's beat-up Chevy was in the carport.

I crept down the cramped hallway toward the bedroom, calling her name again. I paused to knock gently on the bedroom door, then pushed the door open.

I froze. Sprawled on the floor next to her bed was Mabel's pale body. Dressed in shorts and a T-shirt, she had a hypodermic needle stuck in her ankle. I knew she'd overdosed. I knew she was dead and, most important, I knew she didn't normally use drugs.

My brother would've told me if she'd had this kind of problem. After all, he was the local drug dealer.

CHAPTER 14

I WAS LOST. At least for a while. I still had hope of finding Bailey Mae, but Mabel was gone. Gone forever. I just sat in my car, shocked, while the cops and the coroner examined the trailer. I wanted to leave. To be productive. But I couldn't. It was as if I'd been hit in the stomach. I was shattered.

I didn't have time to grieve. People were counting on me. Alice and Bailey Mae needed me. Through some deep sixth sense, I felt like Bailey Mae's disappearance and Mabel's death were somehow connected. I had to swallow my grief and find Bailey Mae. I had to get some goddamn answers.

I headed straight to my brother's house, north of Milton. He always said he liked some distance between work and home. A different set of cops got to harass him. The house and detached garage sat off a long gravel driveway that entered directly onto Route 9. The place was rented, of course, with no neighbors close by.

I didn't see any cars but went to the front door anyway and pounded like I was the lead member of a SWAT team. No answer. He didn't pick up his cell when I called, either. Was he avoiding me? If he was, it was the most common sense he'd shown in a long time.

I came back down to Marlboro and started thinking how crazy it was that my quiet little town had gone off the rails in the last few days. I had to find out why. I would go on the offensive and nothing could stop me.

The search for Bailey Mae started again with a vengeance. I was asking questions about her at the businesses up and down Route 9, showing them the photo of the three strangers that Mabel had taken.

I worked my way all the way down to Newburgh before I found a barber who didn't know anything about Bailey Mae but thought he had trimmed the hair of one of the men in the photo. He said it was just a touch-up on a crew cut. Similar to a military style. The older man had never seen the customer before or since, and the man was alone when he came in to get the trim. That was three days ago.

I stopped at a gas station on North Plank Road, just before it met Route 9, to fill up. I knew the doofus working at the station was one of my brother's regular pot customers. I almost didn't say anything to the gangly twenty-year-old with greasy hair that hung down into his face.

He came out of the station and walked up to me at the pump. "Hey, Mitchum. Where's your brother?"

"Why?" I knew the reason.

"I'm low on weed and someone said he had a new shipment this morning."

I shook my head and couldn't believe how open people were about doing something illegal. I didn't care about pot use; it just annoyed me how much money my brother made doing something that was against the law.

"You heard about my cousin, Bailey Mae?"

He nodded his head. "Natty was by here asking about her yesterday. I haven't seen her."

I held up my phone. "What about any of these three?"

He took a second to study the photo then surprised me by saying, "Yeah, I've seen them a couple times. All three of them were in a dark SUV."

"When was the last time you saw them?"

"Yesterday afternoon."

CHAPTER 15

I WENT BY a couple diners in Newburgh. They were bigger, impersonal places, and the people there didn't know my cousin. They didn't recognize the strangers on my phone. At the second diner, the waitress made me a turkey sandwich because she thought I looked tired and underfed. While I wolfed it down, she refocused her attention on the other tables, leaving me all alone.

As frustrated as I was, it was kinda nice being in Newburgh. It was bigger than our town, and it would be easier to go unnoticed there. That's where I'd stay if I came to the area from somewhere else.

I got nothing from a couple of hotels on the main drag, so I stopped at one tucked off Windsor Highway, called the Red Letter Inn, an obvious nod to *The Scarlet Letter* and adultery. What a nice place.

The clerk barely looked up when I walked through the front door. He was about my age, but much heavier and not particularly chatty. He didn't even grunt as I stepped up and stood by the counter. Behind him, a small TV played *Family Feud*.

Even after I cleared my throat, he didn't acknowledge me. Then I held up a photo of Bailey Mae and said, "I was just wondering if you've seen this girl. She's missing."

The man looked up, scratched the three-day-old growth on his chin, and gave the photograph a cursory examination. His eyes shot up to meet mine briefly, and all he said was "Nope."

I stood there, thinking of different ways to approach this idiot. I dug in my pocket and pulled out my phone, calling up the photograph of the strangers. As I held it up, the man said, "If you're not checking in, you need to be on your way."

I essentially ignored him as I held up the phone and said, "What about these three? Have you seen any of them?"

Now he lifted his head and gave me his full attention. "What do I look like to you? Lost and Found?"

He was big. An inch or two taller than me and at least eighty-five pounds heavier. But I was at the end of my rope. I had to dig deep to be polite as I kept the phone in position and said, "It's really important. Have you seen any of these three people?"

But now he wouldn't even look up.

I pulled a pizza flyer from the edge of the counter, flipped it over, and took a moment to write on it in tiny letters. I slid the flyer across the counter and said, "I guess you know this already."

The big man glanced at the paper, then took a second to try and read it. The letters were so small he had to lean in close and put his head near the counter.

That's when I grabbed his hair and slammed his face into the counter as hard as I could. "It says, 'You're an asshole.'" Then I pulled him right over the counter into the lobby. It was a lot more work than I thought it would be.

I jerked his face up so he was looking at the photo on my phone. I tried to keep my tone even when I said, "Like I was asking, have you seen any of them?"

The big man, who had a trickle of blood running down his face from a broken nose, focused on the photograph, then turned and looked at me sheepishly, saying, "The guy on the left is in room 16. He's driving an older Ford pickup with a snowplow on the front of it. Looks like he's in the military. A little strange, maybe even scary." Then he took a moment, wiped the blood with his bare hand, and said, "But not as scary as you."

CHAPTER 16

I HELPED THE clerk clean up and get settled in his chair. He understood that he wasn't supposed to tell anyone I'd been asking questions. The look on his face told me he'd keep that promise.

It was time to use some of my private investigation skills. This was the one area I was a little weak in, but it was time to try it: surveillance. I was going to conduct my own stakeout at the motel. I parked my car across the highway, at an empty strip mall. No one coming down the road would give a beat-up station wagon a second look.

There was a pickup truck with a professional-looking snowplow attached to the chassis parked directly in front of room 16, which was the last one on the left side of the motel. The truck had been backed into a spot, so I couldn't read the license plate. It didn't matter; I just wanted to see where he'd go.

The whole experience made me feel like a legitimate private investigator. It didn't have anything to do with my knowing the background of someone who needed help and understanding what they were looking for. Often my private investigation business was more about comforting elderly people than actually solving some kind of crime. I never took divorce or cheating cases, and I slept pretty well most nights. Now, in my station wagon, I was waiting for someone who might be dangerous to leave the hotel. Shit was getting real.

CHAPTER 17

I FELT THE weather move in before the snow started to fall. In a few minutes the road was completely blanketed, and more was coming. I looked at my watch and realized it was getting late. I sat, staring at a motel that no one had come out of or gone into in more than three hours. Maybe that's why I don't do much surveillance. It's definitely frustrating.

I couldn't wait any longer. I grabbed my pistol from under the seat, tucked it into my belt, and crossed the road quickly on foot. The motel office was dark, and no one moved anywhere on the property. I checked out the snowplow before I stepped to the door. It was bolted to the truck's chassis and about four feet wide. It looked like it was used to clear small roads or trails. I was trying to think: What kind of trails needed to be cleared around here? The roads were all handled by commercial snowplows, and even though I'd seen a few of these around over the years, none were as expensive and elaborate as this. Usually they were homemade jobs on the front of beat-up pickup trucks that would clear driveways for ten bucks. This was something else.

I moved to the room. There were no lights, and I felt no movement inside when I placed my hand on the door. The moist air made me shiver. At least I think it was the air. I was in uncharted territory professionally. This was nothing like finding out who'd hacked a Facebook account or looking for a husband who had had a few too many drinks.

I couldn't waste any more time. I rapped on the door. In a reasonable fashion at first, then a bit louder. My right hand rested on the butt of the pistol underneath my untucked shirt.

There was no answer, and none of the other customers opened their doors, either.

I looked down at my watch and realized time had gotten away from me. I had to race back to Marlboro to get my papers ready to deliver. But I'd be back to have a talk with the guy at the Red Letter Inn.

CHAPTER 18

IT WAS ONE of the worst mornings I could ever remember. I've seen heavier snowfall, but not this early, when no one was ready for it. Bart had no interest in leaving the comfortable confines of our little house. His flat face looked out the window as I trudged through the snow that had accumulated on my front walk in just a few hours. And the snow was still falling.

As soon as I got to the loading dock and grabbed the papers Nick dropped off, I realized I was just going through the motions. I could do this job with my eyes shut. Almost literally. If it wasn't for the fear of hitting a pedestrian, I might even try it one day. Some days I was in a hurry, and I could be efficient and fast. Today it was just a duty. It was my responsibility to deliver papers, and I was going to do it. I recognized that some of the elderly people on my route depended on the papers for their window to the world. But today it was more about killing time and giving my mind a rest.

As I pulled away from the loading dock in my sagging station wagon, my head was somewhere else. It wasn't somewhere pleasant, but at least it wasn't dwelling on the fact that Mabel was dead and Bailey Mae was still missing.

Just a block from the loading dock, as I pulled up to the closest intersection, I felt a sudden impact. Wham! My whole world started to spin. It was as if I felt the collision before I even heard the deafening crash. My giant old station wagon spun across the icy road, and nothing I did with the steering wheel or brakes seemed to make any difference at all.

As the car started to slow its wild spin, I felt a second impact as the station wagon drove into thick trees on the side of the road. The abrupt stop threw me from the driver's seat into the passenger seat, and my papers spilled from the crates in the rear all over the car.

Somehow I managed to open the passenger door and tumble out onto the cold, hard ground. For the first time, I wondered if the people in the other car were hurt. I struggled to my feet and took a moment to catch my breath and get my bearings. When I looked up, I recognized the vehicle wedged against mine. It was the Ford pickup truck with the snowplow, and it had done a number on my front quarter panel.

As I processed this image, I saw a figure slide out of the driver's side of the pickup. I didn't even know if it was a man or a woman. All I saw was the gun.

I quickly patted my waistline. Damn it. I'd left the pistol in the car. That was a mistake, and now I had to make sure it wouldn't be a fatal one.

I took three quick steps and jumped behind a snowbank, hoping to put some distance between me and my attacker just as he fired two quick shots.

My head jerked as I felt the impact of the second shot. I was hit.

CHAPTER 19

EVEN THOUGH I'D been shot, I somehow managed to low crawl through the brush until I was behind a thicker stand of trees about fifty feet from my disabled car. I leaned up against a tree, taking shallow breaths, and ran my fingers up my forehead and over my scalp. There was some blood, but the bullet must've only grazed me, because my brain was still functioning. I was alive and able to see, and I still understood what it meant to be scared.

Suddenly I realized all that training I got in the Navy hadn't been wasted. It was kicking in. I automatically took in my full surroundings, figured out my best chance of escape, and identified exactly where the danger was coming from. The guy with the gun was now standing at the foot of my car, peering into the dark woods.

I weighed my options. I could turn and run down the path away from the road, but that would give him a clear view and opportunity to shoot me. If I waited, he might walk into the woods searching for me and I'd have a chance to strike if he got close enough. But this guy seemed too professional for that. He was weighing his own options and knew time was on his side.

I needed something, some distraction to make him look away or run toward me. Without conscious thought, my right hand was in a fist and ready for action. But the last thing I wanted to do was get in a fistfight with a guy who had a gun.

Then I heard a noise on the other side of me. It was a low rustle in the brush. I jumped when a figure appeared out of nowhere. My fist almost struck out on its own. Luckily, my brain was able to register who it was.

"Jesus, Al. What are you doing here?" It was a hoarse, harsh whisper, but this was not the time for the older homeless guy to be hanging out.

"It looked like you could use a hand, Mitchum." He slipped off the fleece coat I'd given him a few days earlier and said, "Put this on. You're not used to the cold like I am, and if you lose too much blood the coat will help." Then he peeked at the spot where the man with the gun had stepped farther into the woods. Then Al said, "Be ready to take this guy out."

Before I could even ask him what he was talking about, Al stood up and sprinted, though not all that fast, on the path where the man could see him.

The man took one wild shot then fell into pursuit, immediately running hard right down the middle of the path. He had no idea I was behind a tree that was coming up quickly.

I could hear his footsteps as he raced down the path and was able to time the swing of my arm to clothesline him perfectly. His whole body rose in the air as my arm caught his chest and slid up to his chin. He landed on the ground with a thud.

The gun flew from his hand and landed somewhere in the brush, out of sight. In the few seconds I spent looking for the gun, the man was on his feet and facing me.

He was about my size, with close-cropped brown hair and a tattoo of a teardrop next to his left eye. That meant either he had never been in the military or had been out long enough to get the facial tattoo. Right now that kind of deduction wouldn't help me. He was tough. Too tough for his own good.

He also knew how to fight. His stance gave away nothing, with his fists up to protect his face.

I stepped in and his right leg swung up, blasting me on the right side of my body with a round kick. I deflected some of it with my arm but it still sent a shiver of pain and shock through me. So now I knew he was as fast as lightning, too. I leaned in again and drew a swing of his right fist, which was what I wanted. I dipped slightly and connected with a big punch into his side and was rewarded with the sound of a rib cracking. It might not stop him, but it would make him think every time he moved.

The man backed off slightly but gave no acknowledgment of the blow. We were both breathing hard already and starting to sweat. Most people have no idea how hard it is to actually fight. Adrenaline and physical exertion together can be a bitch.

The man moved forward and threw two front kicks, which I blocked, but they were still powerful. I managed a glancing elbow to his chin, which drove him back and also convinced him he wasn't going to beat me hand to hand.

He kept his distance as he reached into his rear pocket and yanked out a knife. It was the Army Ranger version of mine.

I matched him by jerking my knife from my front pocket and flicking it open, then holding it steady a little in front of me.

The man had a loose grasp on his knife and swung it from side to side as he circled me, looking for an opening.

A trickle of sweat slipped into my eye, but I couldn't wipe it.

The man's lip was bleeding from my elbow strike.

He still said nothing. I had no real idea who had told him to make me the target of this attack. But I wasn't the one who'd regret it. The last thing I wanted to do was stab anyone. Well, second to last. The last thing I wanted to do was die. That meant I had to take serious action.

He swung at me once, with his blade landing on the back of my left hand and cutting me. The next backhand swipe missed me. When he stepped forward again, I knew what he was going to do. As he started his strike again, I raised my bloody left hand and blocked him, and at the same time, I drove my knife straight up into his solar plexus. I heard the sickening sound of the blade piercing the flesh and then driving up.

The man froze mid-strike and just stared at me. Then he took a few staggering steps away as he tried to form a word. Then he collapsed onto the path, holding his wound.

I leaned down and could already feel his pulse had stopped. I must have nicked his heart.

A quick search found no identification on the man. Not that I really needed any. I knew why he had attacked me: I was looking for Bailey Mae and whoever killed the Wilkses—and maybe even poor Mabel.

And I didn't have any real regret for killing this guy unless it kept me from finding Bailey Mae.

CHAPTER 20

I SAT ON the frozen ground, leaning against a tree, trying to catch my breath. I'd used the snow to clean my knife and pack the cut on my left hand. I can't say why. I seemed to be operating on instinct now. It didn't particularly bother me that a few feet away there was a body that I had killed. It had clearly been in self-defense.

A noise to my right made me jump. Then I realized it was Albany Al coming back.

He said, "When this asshole didn't follow me, I figured you'd cleaned his clock." The older man inspected the body more closely. "You don't do anything halfway, do you? Nice job." Now he looked at me and stepped closer, then ran his index finger across my forehead. "Jeez, you're bleeding like a stuck pig. The bullet must have nicked your scalp good." He showed me the blood on his finger. "You are one lucky son of a gun."

All I could do was shrug my shoulders and say, "Yeah, lucky." I didn't feel so lucky. The older man shivered, so I gave him the coat back. I struggled to my feet. My vision was a little blurry.

Al said, "What about him?" He pointed at the body a few feet away.

"I'll worry about explaining him later."

Al held up both hands and said, "I didn't see a thing."

Once on my feet, I really felt the blood. It was a warm sensation in the bracing wind. I nodded good-bye to Al and stumbled back to my car. No one had even driven past the accident yet. It was too early and too nasty out. I had to yank the fender away from my front tire, but the good old station wagon would run. A minute later I was on the highway, headed to the one place I knew I'd be safe. I loved that car. At least for the moment.

My mom's house was a few blocks from mine. I don't care how old you are or what you do in life, your mom's place is always a safe haven. It was the house I grew up in. I stayed there alone with my brother when my mom worked a late shift as a nurse at the emergency room in Newburgh. It was the one place in the world where my troubles never caught up with me.

She was home, and Bart was sitting next to her on the sofa as they both watched a talk show.

She said, "I went to walk Bart and he wanted to come here after." She always made up an excuse to spend a little extra time with my dog. Then she took a closer look and sprang to her feet. "What happened to you? Are you okay?" She was a typical mom at heart.

My mom sent me into the bathroom as she gathered her supplies and made a quick phone call. When she came in, I was already sitting on the stool we'd used for medical treatment since I was a kid. Both Natty and I had most of our injuries tended to here.

Mom had me lean over the sink as she washed my scalp, first with warm water, then peroxide. She parted my thick hair carefully with her fingers and then doused the wound with more peroxide.

I flinched.

My mom said, "Relax—it's not that bad."

"You could be a little more gentle."

"I could be, but this way is faster. I've had too much practice with you. Always pretending to be a SEAL and then all those crazy training courses you invented. You got nicked up all the time." She continued to check my head, then finally said, "This isn't like any of your crazy cuts or bruises. This was a bullet, wasn't it? You going to tell me what happened?"

"I was hoping to avoid that."

"The cut on your hand could be anything, but now I'll assume it was part of a fight." She inspected my left hand, cleaned it easily, and used three butterfly bandages to close it. "You're lucky it's superficial. A deeper cut could have damaged the tendons and affected your grip."

She refocused on my head wound, dumping more peroxide on it and moving my hair again, making me jump. It was like a needle in my head. "I can patch you up a number of different ways."

"But I still won't tell you what happened. I don't want to get you involved."

"Okay then, go bleed to death somewhere else."

"I'm sorry, Mom. But there's something weird going on around town, and it may be related to Bailey Mae. I'm okay—that's why I came here."

"And you didn't want anyone at a hospital asking questions, did you?"

"Yeah, that, too."

She worked miracles with a couple of fancy bandages and some dissolving glue. When it was all done, the bleeding had stopped, and she even combed my hair the way I like it. As she dabbed the dried blood from my forehead, I heard the front door open. I sprang from the stool and reached for my knife. My first thought was that someone had followed me to her house. Exactly what I didn't want to happen.

I stood in the hallway that led to the living room and listened for a moment. I wanted to have an idea of how many people had entered the house. It didn't matter—at this point I was going to deal with all of them at the same time.

Then I heard a male voice that froze me in place.

It was my brother, Natty. That explained the phone call my mom had made.

Crap.

CHAPTER 21

MY MOM WALKED casually past me into the living room, saying, "I called Natty so you could work together to find Bailey Mae. You each have your own strengths and complement each other very well."

I said, "I'm looking for three strangers." I faced my brother and said, "You sell any of your nasty poison to any strangers passing through town?"

Natty said, "I told you I didn't recognize the three people in the photo. I only sell to regular customers."

"You're lying, Natty. Don't be an asshole. Those strangers are tied to Bailey Mae somehow. Bailey Mae and the Wilkses. I know it."

"You don't know shit. You're just a pretend private investigator in a shitty little town. Bailey Mae probably ran away, so we'll find her. I don't have time for any of this shit. At least *I* have a business to run."

"Selling crap to people who can't help themselves? Like the heroin that killed poor Mabel."

Suddenly Natty was indignant. "I never sell heroin and never sold *anything* to Mabel. If she had asked for anything, I would've told you."

I couldn't stand it anymore. My brother's self-righteous excuses for how he made a living caused something to snap inside of me. I punched him right in the face. Hard. The punch was so solid it made *my* head hurt.

To Natty's credit, he wasn't on the floor long. He sprang to his feet and hurled his whole body into me with a vengeance. I stumbled back and we both crashed onto my mother's coffee table, breaking it into a thousand pieces. Magazines flew in every direction.

We ignored our mother's shouts for us to calm down. She even threw in a few curse words, which was rare for her. We tore up her living room, knocking books off the mantel, bending her floor lamp, and flipping her recliner end over end, with my brother's scrawny body lost in the heap. It might've been the loss of blood or the fact that I underestimated my brother's fighting abilities, but going up against him was harder than I would have thought. I guess he had to be in a few fights before he could afford a bodyguard.

We took a moment and backed away from each other when we were both on our feet. I moved to the mantel and caught my breath. He backed toward the kitchen door.

Then I heard an odd sound, like the chime of an old grandfather clock. My brother fell onto the floor, holding his head, as my mom stepped out from behind him with a heavy cast-iron skillet in her hand.

She looked at me with those cool, brown eyes and said, "You want some of this, Bobby?"

I glanced down at my brother, on all fours and shaking his head. "No, ma'am." I didn't want to have anything to do with that skillet.

CHAPTER 22

I TRIED TO be a good brother and helped Natty off the floor and onto the couch. My mom took charge quickly and said, "Bobby, go get the ice bag out of the cupboard and fill it."

That's right. My name is Robert Mitchum. Just like the actor. Named for my grandfather, who was a long-distance trucker, born a few years after the famous Robert Mitchum.

Bart hopped onto the couch just as I came back with the ice bag. He licked Natty's face as my brother slowly regained his senses. His eyes were dilated, which made him look like a cartoon character. My mom, who was acting like she had nothing to do with his present condition, sat on the edge of the couch and gently placed the ice bag on his head.

She said, "You two shake hands and make up."

Way to make your adult sons feel like eight-year-olds, Mom.

Then my mom said, "Are you idiots ready to talk?" She looked at Natty. "I don't care what you do for a living. I'm your mother and I love you. But we need to find Bailey Mae. I'm her great-aunt. So you're going to tell Bobby anything he wants to know, and you're going to do it right now."

Natty mumbled, "Yes, ma'am."

Apparently moms work as well as enhanced interrogation because Natty turned to me and said, "What do you want to know, Mitchum?"

"Have you sold to any strangers?"

"I don't sell to anyone but regular customers."

"Have you seen anything unusual?"

Natty thought about that for a few seconds and said, "The Clagetts have been buying some 'medicinal' pot over the last few weeks. A lot more than usual."

The name didn't spring to mind, so I knew they weren't on my paper route. Then I remembered. "You mean the people who bought those old cabins up in the hills off new Unionville Road?"

"Yeah. But they seem like a nice enough couple."

"Let's head out there and pay them a visit." The fact that we were working together seemed to make my mom happy, even if she was a little worried about what we were doing. She kissed us each on the cheek as I called for Bart to join us. He happily hopped off the couch and trotted toward the door.

CHAPTER 23

WE TOOK MY brother's sports car because it was a little more dependable than my beat-up station wagon. He was clearly uncomfortable with a dog riding unattended in the backseat. It brought a small smile to my face.

We'd been in enough fights with each other since childhood that there was nothing awkward in the aftermath of our last dustup. But as always, Natty was hesitant to talk about his business.

I said, "All I'm asking is to know how you met the Clagetts. No one in town has seen them, except for when they do a grocery run once a week or so."

"I just met them one day and it all worked out."

"Is that how you describe business transactions? They work out?"

"What do you want me to say, Mitchum? We can't all know what we want to do from childhood."

"You noticed my dream didn't work out too well for me."

"At least everyone looks up to you around here. I'm just the drug-dealing brother."

"You can't change that?"

"Not now. Not after all these years. I am what I am, and you're the guy in town everyone counts on. No one cares if you were a SEAL or not. You're still the Man in Marlboro."

I had never considered how my brother felt or knew that he might resent me. It was disconcerting to have to reevaluate my relationship with him, which was based on mutual contempt. He wasn't the shallow narcissist I assumed he was.

We didn't say much more as we turned off Unionville Road up the winding, unnamed gravel path that rose in the foothills and then the steeper inclines of the mountains.

I'd never been back here, just heard about the three cabins that had been part of a resort back in the sixties. The front cabin was clearly the main residence. It had been remodeled, and an asphalt driveway ran up to it. The carport connected the detached garage to what appeared to be a three-bedroom building. Behind it on each side were smaller cabins that were more run-down and had no carports.

A Ford sedan was parked in the driveway. As we approached the front door, I touched the hood of the car to feel if it had been driven recently. It was ice-cold.

I let Bart out of the car to get some exercise and do his business. There were a few patches of grass around the house, but the snow got thicker heading up the hills.

The front porch creaked as we carefully stepped up to the door. This time I'd thought ahead and had my pistol tucked in my pants.

My knife was safely in my pocket. I was tired of getting surprised and abused by strangers.

Natty tapped on the door like we were visiting a relative. There was no immediate answer so I pounded on it with my left fist. When we got no answer for a second time, I tried the handle. It was locked.

The deadbolt hadn't been turned, so I pulled out my Navy knife and flicked it open with my thumb. The sound of it clicking into place caught Natty's attention, and when I wedged it into the door to jimmy the lock, he started protesting.

Once the door was open, I stepped inside.

From the porch, Natty said, "Are you crazy? We could get arrested for this."

"That's funny coming from a drug dealer."

"With two convictions. I can't risk a simple breaking and entering. They'd send me upstate for five years."

I walked farther into the house, looking for any clues about the people who lived there.

Reluctantly, Natty followed me inside. "We could both be killed. Is that what you want?"

I didn't turn to face him when I said, "All I want is to find Bailey Mae."

When I got to the rear of the cabin I noticed Bart in the backyard. He was sniffing something and interested in it.

I went out the back door and Natty followed. When I got to Bart, I kneeled down to pat his back and said, "What did you find, boy?" That's when I realized there were several sets of tracks in the snow from the rear of the cabin heading up into the hills. It was a well-used path and the latest set of tracks was fairly fresh.

Without a word I started the trek up the hill, following the tracks. Natty started to protest, but then just followed me.

CHAPTER 24

THE TRAIL WAS firm, with the snow piled on either side. I was surprised how steep the incline was and felt my heart rate start to climb as I kept a steady march up the path. After a few hundred yards I was glad we'd left Bart on the porch of the cabin. He seemed happy to let us go on our way, and I knew he'd be safe there.

Natty started to complain as the path entered the thick woods and continued to go higher. Every once in a while I could see remnants of the old resort and where a road off to the side followed the path. The road would be tough to navigate in winter, but in summer it seemed wide enough for any kind of vehicle. Unless you had a snowplow—then it could be open year-round.

The cold wind whipped down off the mountaintop and made me shiver even though I was working pretty hard. Natty's breath became more ragged as his lifestyle started to catch up with him.

Natty said, "What are we doing out here in this frozen tundra?"

"You know exactly what we're doing: looking for Bailey Mae."

"You don't think this is a little crazy? We go from asking people if they've seen a missing teenager to trekking through the woods behind someone's cabin? This seems pretty thin and a waste of time."

"You don't have to be here."

"Mom said I did. Besides, I can't leave you out here alone. I just think our time could be spent more efficiently. There's nothing out here. We're following some kind of old hunting trail."

We cleared a rise in the trail and stopped, amazed by what we saw.

In front of us, about a hundred yards away, was a small cabin with the lights on and smoke coming from the chimney. I had never seen it or heard anyone mention a cabin all the way back here. It was more like a shack, hastily constructed to protect people from the weather.

I had to look at Natty and say, "What were you saying about nothing being back here?"

Then Natty mumbled, "Maybe you *are* a good investigator."

CHAPTER 25

WE CAREFULLY MOVED around to the front of the shack, which had a window on each side of the only door. As we got closer, we could see one guy inside, sprawled out on the couch with a computer on his lap. He was in his thirties and kind of pudgy but looked like he'd been in pretty good shape at one time. Now he just looked like a couch potato. The fireplace made the room look cozy, and for some reason it pissed me off.

Natty eased up beside me and took a peek.

Then I realized what was on a plate next to him on the couch: a piece of Bailey Mae's coffee cake.

I pulled Natty away from the window and said in a low voice, "Ever see him before?"

Natty was sheepish and finally stammered, "No, well, I mean, maybe. I think."

"Natty," I growled.

"Yeah. I guess I sold him some weed once."

I glared at him.

"Maybe a few times. And a little coke. And some pills. That

ADHD shit." He paused and cocked his head like a puppy. "What's the look for? Any good businessman needs to diversify."

"I thought you only sold pot to regular customers."

Natty shrugged. "After the first time he *was* a regular customer. And just how am I supposed to remember everything and everyone?"

I looked back at the cabin and crept toward it with Natty close behind. I pulled my pistol from under my shirt.

Then he grabbed my arm and said, "Wait, what are we doing? Do you have any idea what kind of trouble we could be in for using a gun in a home invasion?"

"Yeah, I do. But this guy might lead us to Bailey Mae." I jerked my arm away from Natty and stepped up to the door.

CHAPTER 26

THE DOOR WAS unlocked. I was disappointed I didn't get to kick in anything in a dramatic fashion. We rushed inside just the same. The effect was perfect. Couch Potato Man stared in stunned silence for a moment then tried to get to his feet, knocking the plate with Bailey Mae's coffee cake onto the floor.

The sight of my gun pointed at him slowed the man down. Now he eased back onto the couch and said, "You scared the shit out of me." He looked at Natty and said, "I'm all paid up with you. What's the problem?"

I said, "Where's the girl? Where's Bailey Mae, you son of a bitch?"

Couch Potato Man said, "I have no idea what you assholes are talking about. Who the hell is Bailey Mae?"

Then he stood up. That was his mistake. I was pissed off and he was in range, so I popped him in the face with my left fist, keeping the gun pointed at him with my right hand. Although I felt it in the cut on the back of my hand, I was glad to get off a good, solid punch that knocked him back. He tumbled across the couch and landed on the hard floor. He immediately covered himself with his hands like there was a gang about to pummel him.

I was breathing hard as I stood over the man with the pistol still in my hand. "Don't make me ask you again. Where is she?"

Couch Potato Man kept his head down with his hands shielding his face. "Please don't hit me," he whined as he scooted away from me, toward the couch. He sat up with his back against the couch but kept his hands up like he was terrified. Was this some kind of act? Was he buying time? I didn't care. I needed answers.

Couch Potato Man said, "I didn't do anything to anyone. I don't know anyone named Bailey Mae. I'm basically camping here. Squatting."

I noticed his eyes shift to the right, looking past me. About the same time I caught a movement outside the window. Before I could turn, the door burst open.

Natty squawked like a bird.

I spun and found a gun in my face. My eyes ran up the barrel to the owner. It was the woman from Mabel's photo.

CHAPTER 27

THE MAN STANDING next to her said, "Put the gun on the ground. Do it now."

That was a command from someone who had either military or police experience. I slowly bent down to place the gun on the floor, but I kept my eyes on the couple who'd stepped inside the shack. The man was also from the photo. He was lean and in good shape, with close-cropped hair. The woman was about five foot ten and had straight black hair that hung to her neck, with very little styling. She had sharp lines to her face and didn't look like she took much shit.

I didn't make any sudden movements and did nothing to cause alarm or force them to shoot. But as I stood back up, I felt a strong emotion—and it wasn't fear. It was anger. These people thought they could do whatever they wanted in my town. They probably took Bailey Mae, and now they were pointing guns at my brother and me.

Natty could never keep his mouth shut. As a kid he was fearless, even though he didn't have the muscle to back it up. Sure enough, he said, "Just who the hell are you guys?"

Now Couch Potato Man was standing up behind us, no doubt looking forward to some payback. But like the other two, Couch Potato Man was now focused on Natty.

Natty continued. "I sold this slacker some weed. He didn't seem so bad. What the hell is your problem?" He jabbed his finger at the couple.

While the armed couple focused their attention on my idiot brother, I eased my right hand into my front pocket. No one even noticed. My brother could hold people's attention.

He said, "If you assholes think you can move in on my territory, I got news for you."

I made my move. My Navy knife was out and flicked open in a heartbeat, while they all stared at my brother like he was some kind of evangelist who had gone insane on the pulpit. I was close, but not quite close enough. That forced me to try something crazy, but this whole situation was crazy. I leaned into it and threw the knife. Hard. It hit the woman in the upper chest, knocking her back, and she staggered from shock.

Her male companion fired as I moved. The round went wide and I was on him before he could pull the trigger again. I was bigger and had momentum. He went down and his pistol flew across the floor. I put him in an arm lock, making him gasp in pain.

When Couch Potato Man moved toward the pistol, Natty took action. He threw a solid elbow into the man's chin. Nice. Then he shoved the man back onto the couch. Right where a couch potato belonged.

We had no time to waste. I twisted my body and broke the other man's arm.

The woman was on the floor in shock.

Natty picked up the loose pistol. "Now this is what I'm talking about." He pointed the gun at Couch Potato Man.

I rolled away and onto my feet. My anger came out in a scream. "Where's Bailey Mae?!"

CHAPTER 28

NATTY LOOKED LIKE he enjoyed holding the gun on Couch Potato Man. I had other things to do. The man on the floor, closest to me, was moaning and holding his arm. The woman by the door was barely conscious. Now I had both her pistol and mine.

I looked at Natty and said, "Pull off a couple lamp cords and grab some rags from the kitchen. Let's tie these jerks up."

Natty hesitated at first, then tucked the gun in his belt and ripped the cord from a floor lamp, then the cords from some old blinds. The cords and a couple of longer dishrags made for decent restraints as we tied the men's hands behind their backs. The man with the broken arm whimpered. Then, for good measure, I tied each man's ankles together with a lamp cord. That would keep them from having any ideas about running.

I carefully examined the woman on the floor, then eased my knife out of her chest and used a dish towel and duct tape over her wound to stem the bleeding. She moaned and seemed to be in and out of consciousness. Then her eyes focused.

"Get me to a hospital." Even in this state she was scary.

I gave her a smile and said, "No problem. Just tell me where Bailey Mae is."

She looked puzzled.

"My cousin, fourteen, cute, brown hair." I took time to look at each of the other assholes. Couch Potato Man wouldn't meet my eyes. The other man said, "I don't know what you're talking about, but she needs help. Now."

"So do I."

Then I thought of a way to make them talk.

CHAPTER 29

I KNEW NATTY would never look at me the same way again, but we had to get some answers. I got his attention and said, "Come on, let's drag them all outside."

"Outside? Are you crazy? It's freezing out there."

"Exactly."

The snow was still coming down hard and the wind had picked up. None of them had coats on. They weren't ready to be stuck outside. That made me realize the couple with the guns had come to the shack from somewhere close.

Natty was silent as we dragged them out the front door. I pulled the two men about twenty feet from the shack, then tightened the cord tied around their ankles so they couldn't get loose or walk. Natty was careful with the woman as he eased her onto the snow a few feet from the men.

Couch Potato Man rolled so he could face me. He had a hitch in his voice when he said, "You can't do this."

"Apparently I can." I calmly took Natty by the arm and led him back into the shack. The door was open so they could clearly see inside. A little psyops, just like the military would use.

Once inside I stoked the fire, found a turkey sub in the refrigerator, and gave half to Natty, then had him plop down on the couch within view of our hosts.

I said in a low voice, "Let them see you eating."

I poked around the shack. Aside from Bailey Mae's coffee cake, there was nothing of any interest. The laptop Couch Potato Man was working on was a high-end model with a tough outer body, and the screen was secured by a password.

When I was done, I grabbed my half of the sub and sat down next to Natty. Both of the men stared at me from outside. I toasted their discomfort with my sub and gave them a smile.

CHAPTER 30

NATTY SURPRISED ME with his compassion. I didn't realize drug deal-ers were so concerned with other people's needs.

He said, "We can't let that woman die out there."

"She knows how to save herself."

Things were quiet outside. It looked like the woman had passed out. Even though I wouldn't admit it out loud, I was worried, too. After another minute I stood up and casually strolled outside. Even in my coat I felt the bite of the wind. The guy who seemed to be in charge, the one who surprised us with the woman, spoke directly to me.

"You're in way over your head, Mr. Mitchum."

That got my attention.

I said, "Look who's talking. The guy I have in custody. But I'm honored you know my name."

The man kept calm. "Don't wash out here like you did in San Diego with the SEALs. Just walk away from the whole thing. You'll thank me later."

"I'll thank you right now. I'll even let you go when you tell me where my cousin is. I'm impressed you know about my military record. You must have some decent connections."

The man wasn't falling for any of my banter and gave nothing away, but Couch Potato Man was looking increasingly scared and was now shivering uncontrollably.

I stood up and stretched. "Think I might be ready for a nap." I turned toward the shack. That was all Couch Potato Man needed to break.

I took one step and he shouted, "Wait, wait. Get us inside and I'll tell you what you need to know."

CHAPTER 31

THE FREEZING WIND had hurt my exposed face so I knew it had done a number on these three thugs. By the time Couch Potato Man made his plea, I was concerned about leaving the trio out there much longer. I was tempted to take him up on his offer and drag him back inside before he talked, but I knew it could be a ploy. These guys had already proven to be shifty and more cunning than me. Now I had to turn ruthless just to get answers. I needed to hear what he had to say, and I needed to hear it outside. Now.

I looked at Natty and finally said, "Carry the woman inside and cover her with a blanket on the couch."

For a change, Natty did exactly what I asked. He even lifted the woman off the ground completely, instead of dragging her. I had to trust him and not take my eyes off the other two as he secured her inside.

The guy tied to Couch Potato Man gave me a hard stare and said, "You're making a mistake. It's not too late to just walk away."

"If that was true, you wouldn't be trying so hard to convince me. You know we're about to blow whatever you're up to and the couch potato here is gonna tell me all about it unless he wants to freeze into a statue."

The guy looked at Couch Potato Man and said, "Don't say a goddamn word, Becker."

Becker, one more piece of information to file away. But I liked the name Couch Potato Man better. It was more descriptive.

I leaned down and used my knife to cut the cord around the men's legs. When Natty popped his head out, I motioned for him to bring the other man inside as well. It had the right psychological effect on Couch Potato Man.

He was now shivering uncontrollably as ice formed in his eyebrows and his face changed to a dark shade of blue.

"You better start talking," I said.

He hesitated as his eyes drifted past me to the path that disappeared into the woods on the hills.

I rose to my feet, like I was out of patience. Actually, I really was done with this whining fake tough guy. The woman was safe, and I had no more time to waste. I turned and took one step before I heard him say, "Okay, okay."

He had the manic speech of a guy who was not only scared but maybe on too much speed or meth. No wonder I found these guys through a drug dealer. What else was there to do up here so isolated?

"Was there a girl here? Fourteen, cute, brown hair?"

Couch Potato Man shrugged and said, "I guess."

This time I grabbed him by the throat. It felt like I was holding a block of ice. But it got his attention.

He nodded his head. "She was here, she was here, but I'm not sure where she went. She wasn't supposed to see anything. No one was. It was just a misunderstanding."

I looked at the cabin in the wilderness and said, "Why *are* you here? What the hell are you asswipes doing?"

"Look, I answered your question. Do you want to find the girl or not?"

I was tired of being jerked around. I had a lot of questions that needed to be answered. I lost it. I pulled my pistol from my belt and shoved it in the creep's face. The barrel pushed against his nose, making him look like a terrified Porky Pig.

Couch Potato Man knew I was serious and called out, "Try the trail, try the trail." He turned his head and I followed his eyes along the trail that led into the woods. "Straight up the path a ways. She might be up there."

I realized this guy was like the devil. He could tell you what you wanted to hear, but it could also be a lie. The whole setup gave me a bad feeling.

I left the man on the ground as I released my grip and stood up. I said, "Tell me what you're doing here. I don't care what happens to you or the others, I need answers."

Couch Potato Man looked up at me and said, "Who the hell are you anyway?"

"Just a guy worried about his family. Now talk."

"I told you, mister, follow the path and you'll find out every-thing you need to know."

Then he told me a little about what I might find in the hills. And it didn't sound inviting.

CHAPTER 32

WHEN I ENTERED the cabin, shoving Couch Potato Man in front of me, the other guy who had shown up with the woman said, "You better not have said anything, Becker."

Couch Potato Man just shrugged, still shivering.

Natty and I spent a few minutes securing the men into chairs. The duct tape came in handy, and I couldn't resist using a small square on each man's mouth. They looked like cartoon characters with so much tape and the cords holding them in place. The man who'd come in with the woman was silently furious. I knew he was a guy to watch out for. Hopefully this would go the way I planned. Otherwise he would be an issue later. Men like that never forget and never forgive. Not only had I screwed up his little operation, I had embarrassed him in front of his comrades. He watched me and calculated what he could do to me later.

The woman was unconscious on the couch, and there was no way she was faking it, so we left the shack and hustled up the trail that Couch Potato Man had told me about.

The walk gave me a few minutes to think. Couch Potato Man

had said to follow the trail, but he wasn't clear about exactly what we'd find. That was never a good plan to follow in a situation like this, but I had no choice. I hated the idea of losing Bailey Mae more than anything.

After almost four hundred yards and a steeper than expected incline, I started to understand more of what Couch Potato Man was talking about. I almost ran right past it, hidden in the side of the hill. Instead, I skidded to a stop on the icy path and stared as Natty moved in beside me.

He mumbled, "What the . . . ?"

"Exactly," was all I could say as I stood mesmerized.

An entrance to a subterranean complex sat before us. I couldn't take my eyes off it. I stepped forward and touched the black steel frame around the matching door. It was built solidly into the side of the hill. A bunker, just like Couch Potato Man had told me about. Freezing temperatures are helpful like that.

I paused, considering what could lie beyond the door. More important, I wondered *who* could be waiting beyond the door. That was a question I should have asked the freezing Couch Potato Man, but I was learning as I went. I had to admit my mistakes.

The door was ajar just a crack. This was where the armed couple had come from. I shoved it open and stood back with the gun in my hand. There was a strong odor of unwashed flesh coming from the dimly lit corridor carved directly from the rock.

Natty said, "I guess he was telling the truth." He reached up and ran his finger across the rough walls.

The corridor was more of a tunnel with a ceiling that hung just above my head, giving me a jolt of claustrophobia. Sounds carried in a place like this, but that was a two-way street. I didn't want to alert anyone who might be down here, so I signaled Natty to keep quiet.

A low yellow light came from the end of the corridor. I took each step like I was walking on rice paper. I was nervous, but knew the answers I needed were somewhere ahead of me.

I marveled at the construction and realized it was extraordinarily well built. What the hell was a bunker doing here? How did they build it without the town talking about it? Unless it was already here and someone just spruced it up. Maybe it had something to do with the resort or even a bomb shelter from the fifties.

As soon as we stepped inside, I could feel nominal heat. Low-level lighting cast shadows on the walls. I found myself swallowing hard. As I moved forward, Natty was right behind me. He didn't care if he showed his fear. I could see a small room up ahead with a cot and some stacked supplies.

My heart pounded in my chest.

As we approached the room, Natty bumped an electrical box built into the wall of the bunker. That's when we heard a man's voice. He was somewhere lost in the shadows of the supply room. In the stillness his words startled me like an air horn. He said, "What was Becker worried about? Nothing, as usual?"

Then I saw him. Sitting on a stool, writing in a ledger. A man in his mid-forties, as bald as the old Mr. Clean from the commercials. He was built like him, too.

Natty and I just stared at him until he looked up. I started to bring my gun up as the man burst off the stool and barreled into us, knocking us onto the ground. Poor Natty acted as a cushion and was trapped beneath the man and me.

The man punched me in the side of the head. I returned an elbow, but at this close range, it had little effect. Natty yelped beneath us.

This was going to be a real fight.

CHAPTER 33

THE BALD MAN was incredibly strong and moved like a cat. He had shoved two full-grown armed men off their feet without using a weapon. The impact and punch had knocked me senseless for a moment, and I'd lost track of my gun, which was somewhere on the hard, roughly finished rock floor.

I had a grip on both of the man's wrists and was trying to slide off Natty so he could breathe and maybe help me in the fight. As we struggled, the powerful man jerked his right hand free, and I felt him reach toward his leg. I figured he had a gun secured somewhere on his ankle. I had already felt the bite of his combat boot as it ripped down my shin.

I tried to stop him from reaching for what I thought was a gun. Then I learned I was wrong. It was worse.

He had a knife—and not a commemorative folding one like mine. This was a full-length, straight-edged combat knife like one a Marine would carry. He got it free of its scabbard and brought it up with his right hand to drive it into my throat.

I blocked the blade and parried it to the side. I could feel the steel edge as it grazed my ear and made a click against the hard floor.

The man twisted on top of me, bringing the knife back up. A knife is a weapon of terror and it was working. I couldn't take my eyes off it. I had almost nothing left.

Then he slid up higher to get his weight into his next thrust. That's when instinct kicked in. My left hand was trapped between us. I shoved it lower, then squeezed. Squeezed with all the power in my hand around his testicles. His face registered surprise, then pain. He rolled to get away, but I held on. Then it was Natty's turn to surprise me.

As soon as we were off him and lying on the hard rock floor, Natty swung his pistol and struck the man square in the face with the butt of the gun. The blow was phenomenal and shattered the man's nose. The fight went out of him at once, and he dropped the knife.

I had to lie on my back and stare at the low ceiling while taking in a few breaths. Between the closed-in space and the knife, I was a little freaked-out. I sat up and scanned the room to make sure he was the only sentinel. I also noticed that there was almost no noise. Our struggle had brought a stillness to the bunker.

The man was laid out, with a broken nose and split upper lip, but he was breathing.

Natty whispered, "What do we do with him?"

"For now we leave him right here. We've gotta search this place for Bailey Mae."

CHAPTER 34

WE LEFT THE man right where he was on the floor of the small supply room and kept moving carefully through the dark hallway, which felt like it was closing in around us and suffocating me.

Across from the supply room there was a long panel of heavy metal grating. It took a moment to realize why the grating enclosed the separate rooms: they were cells, each about the size of a large walk-in closet. The tight pattern of the metal obscured our view, but I could make out the outline of a person in each damp cell.

What the hell?

One cell was open and empty. Inside was a table with straps on it and a water hose connected to a faucet. The sight made my skin crawl and sent a wave of panic through me. Bailey Mae shouldn't be anywhere near a place like this. Whatever this place was.

The people inside the cells started to move forward when they realized Natty and I weren't their regular jailers. They rattled the doors, and a few said, "Please, out" or "Open."

I had a bad feeling about the whole situation and realized

we'd stumbled onto something way out of our experience. It was like we had stepped into hell. We were underground and these people were clearly being tormented. Natty was so close he bumped against me with every step. Even though it was cold, I was sweating, and the sweat stung my eyes and blurred my vision. The odor of human waste hit me. I ran my fingers over the ceiling to make sure it wasn't getting lower or narrowing as we walked.

I called out Bailey Mae's name several times but got no response.

As we moved, I inspected the doors to the cells and saw that they didn't need a key. Instead, at the top and the bottom of each door there was a latch that could only be opened from the outside.

As I started to open the first door, Natty tried to stop me and said, "We don't know why they're locked up. They could be dangerous."

"More dangerous than the asshole that just tried to stab me? Don't be an idiot, Natty. Help me."

"But what if they're criminals?"

"Who locks up criminals in a cave? This isn't Pakistan. It's upstate New York, for God's sake."

The latches took some effort, but we managed to muscle the doors open. None of the captives jumped up to get out of the cells immediately. They just stared at us like they didn't understand what we were doing.

As we worked our way down the hall, I kept asking, "Is there a young girl here?" I noticed all of the prisoners were men and seemed to have trouble with English.

There were no clear answers, and we continued to move forward as we picked up our pace. I screamed, "Bailey Mae!" and looked into each cell.

My hope was fading. What nightmare had we wandered into?

CHAPTER 35

AT ABOUT THE sixth cell, a man in his mid-fifties stepped into the hallway. He was short and frail with streaks of gray in his unwashed hair.

The man said in accented English, "My name is Hassan. I believe the girl is down there." He pointed toward the end of the corridor.

I broke into a run and came to the last cell. It was darker this far down the hall, and when I looked in the cell no one was inside. My heart sank. Then I caught just a hint of movement in the shadows and heard a tiny voice.

"Mitchum? Is that you?"

I stared into the dark cell.

Bailey Mae sat up and a beam of weak light caught her brown hair.

Frantically, I pulled the top latch down, then jerked hard on the lower one and felt the door give. As soon as I had the cell open, Bailey Mae rose from a metal cot and fell into my arms as I stepped inside. I couldn't stop the sob of relief that came out.

She was weak, but alive.

Natty finished releasing everyone from the cells. There were about fifteen, all men. I noticed they were all dark-skinned and probably Middle Eastern. They all turned and started to gather in the supply room. As I hustled down there with Bailey Mae still in my arms, I realized they were surrounding the bald man Natty had hit in the face. The man was conscious now and in a low crouch.

It was clear as they crowded around the hunched jailer that these men were not happy with how they'd been treated. One of them picked up the combat knife that was on the ground nearby.

Although I didn't give a shit about this guy, something inside me made me speak up. "Hold on. We need to let the authorities deal with this jerk-off."

The man who had told me where Bailey Mae was, Hassan, turned and said, "There is nothing they could do to this man that would give us vengeance."

"Just the same, we're gonna lock him in one of the cells until we figure out what's going on." I handed Bailey Mae to Natty so I could face the crowd. I hadn't bothered to find my gun, and although I was the biggest guy there, I realized the numbers were not in my favor.

I said, "He'll be secure in a cell until the police can come."

A man in his forties with a scar on his left cheek and a beard that meandered down his neck stepped forward and spoke with a heavy accent. "I deal with him." His smile gave away his intentions.

"No, I said we'll let the authorities deal with him."

But that did not sit well with the crowd.

CHAPTER 36

ONCE WE SECURED the bald man in a cell, I faced the former captives. Natty leaned in and said, "We gotta get out of here."

Bailey Mae said, "As long as we take everyone with us."

Natty looked surprised and said, "We can't be responsible for all of these men."

Even in her weakened state, Bailey Mae was resolute. "They're my friends. Hassan helped me and kept talking to me. I'm not leaving without them."

Not only did I not want to argue, but she made sense. If something went wrong and the people in the cabin took control again, these poor men wouldn't have a chance. My only concern was the weather and their weakened condition. I considered the hike back and decided the downward slope to the cabin would help them.

Bailey Mae just gave me a look and I knew that, no matter what, we were bringing these men with us.

I said in a loud voice, "All right, everyone. We have to hike down the hill and it's cold outside. Find whatever you can to wrap yourself up in. Does anyone feel like they can't make it?" I scanned the little crowd and realized there was no way anyone would speak up. They would make it down the hill if their legs were broken.

Natty and I carried Bailey Mae from the bunker and headed back to the cabin, leading the slow-moving group of former captives. I wanted to make the trip as quickly as possible because the men weren't dressed for the weather, but not so fast that they couldn't keep up.

Bailey Mae felt like a feather in my arms but somehow found the strength to hold me around the neck as if she were a rodeo rider. When we reached the cabin, I could tell by Bailey Mae's reaction she knew all three of the people we had tied up. Depending on what she told me, there was a chance I was going to kill one or more of them.

The men crowded into the living room and most of them immediately sat down, exhausted from the hike down from the bunker. They clearly recognized all three of our captives.

Bailey Mae sat next to me at the kitchen counter as I fumbled with my phone to call 911. I told the operator we needed police and fire rescue and that we had multiple injuries. I figured that would get them moving fast. Explaining our exact location was a little more difficult. She wasn't sure who I was, but after I told them to check with Timmy Jones, the dispatcher didn't ask any more questions. I wasn't about to try to explain who my fifteen new friends were. I still didn't know.

It was clear both of the thugs we'd secured in the chairs had struggled and failed to get out of the binds that held them. All I could do was look at them and say, "Nice try, assholes." I had a million questions, but I didn't think these guys were ready to talk, short of me dragging them outside again.

I stepped over to the couch and checked the woman, who was now conscious and staring in disbelief at the men who had been her captives. It looked like she would live, and that was good enough for me.

I took a man's heavy coat from a hanger near the door and slipped it around Bailey Mae. As I leaned in, I said, "Don't worry, kid. Help is on the way."

Natty and I dragged the two chairs with the men tied to them all the way into the kitchen, away from the freed men. I ripped the tape off their mouths, but neither spoke immediately. The man in charge just shook his head and mumbled, "I won't forget you, Mitchum."

"Wish I could forget you and this whole nightmare."

"But you won't be able to. No matter what happens. No matter how this all plays out, I'll still be thinking of how you screwed things up and what I'll do to you the first chance I get."

"What, exactly, did I screw up?"

"A chance to make a difference. A chance to really protect the country. Instead, we're no better off than we were before September 11."

"You really believe that, don't you?"

"Someone has to."

"How does torturing a few scared men protect anything?"

"You don't get it, do you, Mitchum? It's all connected. The Middle East, Europe, the US; every action has a consequence.

From supporting Hamas to supplying electrical parts that could be used to bring down a jet. It's all connected and you're gonna have to live with the guilt when shit happens because of what you did here."

I was tired of this guy. "How does kidnapping a little girl protect anything?"

"I didn't say we were perfect. Accidents happen, people make mistakes. One day I hope you're collateral damage to an accident."

I just stared at him as I fantasized about shooting this creep in the head, but I wasn't like him. Thank God I wasn't like him and I had to know there was a difference between us. I gave him a smirk, then turned my back on him. I hoped for good.

When I stepped out of the kitchen, Bailey Mae reached out to take my hand.

She pulled me closer and whispered in my ear, "I knew you'd find me."

That one sentence, those few words, made all this worthwhile. But I was still confused, and confusion doesn't sit well with a guy like me. I like to see a problem and tackle it. Head-on. This was a puzzle, and I didn't see a clear answer. I straightened up. The freed men were all looking at me to see what my next move would be.

I looked over at Couch Potato Man, who had remained unusually quiet. I said, "You guys feel tough locking up a little girl?"

He didn't say a word.

Bailey Mae tugged on my arm and waited for me to lean down so her mouth was close to my ear. She said, "I saw it, Mitchum."

"Saw what?"

She nodded at Couch Potato Man. "I was delivering my coffee cakes to the Wilkses and I saw that man shoot them. They worked with these people. Mr. Wilks found this place for them. I heard them argue about money, and Mr. Wilks said he'd tell the media about it. That's when that guy shot them. Bang, bang, without any hesitation. I was so scared I couldn't move. He turned around with the pistol in his hand, and the only thing I did was put down my coffee cakes and freeze."

Now I definitely didn't regret anything I had done to the man tied in the chair.

CHAPTER 37

ON THE OTHER side of the cabin, the former captives sat in a group as the realization that they had been rescued sank in. Each man accepted it in his own way. One younger man, maybe only twenty, leaned against the wall, sobbing quietly. Several others were smiling or laughing with the joy of being free and out of that hellhole. Two middle-aged men eyed Couch Potato Man and my other two prisoners with palpable malice. I worried that I might have to step over there just to keep the peace, but I had no doubt that these thugs had earned the hatred of the captives.

I tried to imagine being caged in that smelly hole and wondering if I'd ever get out. The idea gave me the willies. It made me realize everything I'd miss. My family, even my brother, was important to me, but so was the whole town. It made me angry to think that someone tried to take that from these men. I almost considered letting them take their revenge. Instead, I plopped silently onto a stool by the kitchen.

Neither of the men we'd subdued looked scared. They didn't even look worried. I didn't like it. The man who had threatened me took in the whole room, listening to what was being said, and seemed to be calculating something. What he was calculating I couldn't say, but the gears were turning in his head.

None of us spoke as we waited for the cavalry to arrive. Bailey Mae stayed close to me, sitting on a stool next to the breakfast bar in the kitchen. I noticed she wanted Hassan near her as well. Despite all the mind-blowing shit going on, my main concern was Bailey Mae. She was a strong girl and had done a phenomenal job just staying alive. She was also the key to justice for these men. At least one of the men in custody was guilty of a double homicide. Could they have somehow murdered Mabel as well?

Timmy Jones was the first to come jogging up the path, calling his exact location into his radio. He skidded to a stop at the front door and took in the scene before looking at me and saying, "Are you guys all right?" Then he looked farther inside the cabin and said, "Who are all these people? Is this some kind of immigrant smuggling ring?"

I stepped outside the cabin and gave him a very quick rundown, only hitting the high points. I told him about the bunker complex, the man locked up in the cell, how we'd released the prisoners, the fight in the cabin. Other than that, I had no real answers yet. But I intended to get them. I wondered if the blank stare he was giving me was similar to the one that had been on my face an hour earlier.

I said, "I know it sounds unbelievable, but you'll see the bunker and the cells soon enough. And Bailey Mae positively identified a man inside as the one who shot the Wilkses. She was an eyewitness."

Timmy tried to hide his shock by looking up the path, then back at me, saying, "I never even knew this was back here."

Within minutes, more patrol cars arrived and someone figured out how to access the path so a rescue vehicle with four-wheel drive could make it up from the lower cabins.

I grabbed Timmy by the arm and said, "There's a bald guy locked in one of the cells. He attacked me with a knife. Natty was a witness. The guy is strong and knows how to fight, so be careful when you or your people deal with him."

A few minutes later, two deputies brought the bald man down in handcuffs. One of the deputies had a bloody lip, and his shirt was pulled out of his pants. The bald man had a red mark across his face where someone had used an expandable baton to get his attention. They tied him up with the others in the kitchen.

Bailey Mae was still sitting next to Hassan. The man was weak and had started shivering. I wasn't sure what else to do, so I draped a blanket over him. The cabin was getting busier as more blankets were brought in for the other men. No one had been transported yet, and there was a great deal of confusion about what to do with everyone.

I leaned in close to Hassan and said in a low voice, "What the hell is going on?"

He shook his head. "I live in Marblehead, just outside of Boston. About a month ago, two men questioned me at my convenience store. They said I was aiding terrorists by donating money to a relief fund. That same night I found myself here, being interrogated." He looked around the room and said, "The man over there"—he pointed to a figure on the floor with a blanket over him—"lives in Yonkers and was brought here just last week. We were all questioned over and over."

Natty had crept up behind us and said, "By Americans?"

The man nodded solemnly.

Natty said, "The FBI?"

The man shrugged. "The bald man on the kitchen floor is in charge. He used the table and water hose to scare us. It felt like I was drowning. He would ask the same questions over and over. He's the one all of my friends want to kill right now."

Right then I realized the people doing this were private contractors. Most of them had been in the military and were hired by some firm contracted by the US government to handle the interrogation and housing of potential threats to national security.

This was bullshit.

CHAPTER 38

EVEN THOUGH IT was the middle of the night, more emergency vehicles had come up the path. There was no doubt the truck with the snowplow had kept this path clear.

I stood at the cabin's front door and watched as a string of vehicles rolled into the open space by the narrow road. They were all black SUVs, and I knew something was up.

A tall woman slid out of the rear seat of the second SUV and I heard her say to a deputy, "Who's in charge here?" She was directed to Timmy, who was standing near me, helping figure out how badly each prisoner needed medical attention.

The woman marched directly to Timmy and flipped open her ID case, showing that she worked for Homeland Security. As if to emphasize her position of power, six men and two women climbed out of the other vehicles, each armed with a different type of automatic weapon. I immediately recognized the unique silhouettes of M16s and saw some more exotic weapons, like a Heckler & Koch, as well as a tricked-out Winchester sniper rifle. None of the agents wore fatigues. Instead, they had on mismatched ski vests and jeans, creating the illusion that they were just like everyone else. But they weren't. They were all in their mid-thirties and in good shape, and each knew to keep watch on a different area. It was clear they'd had military training.

Timmy was shaken by the show of force and waved the fire rescue people back to their jobs. He even called out, "Let's make sure we have all of these men transported in the next twenty minutes." He turned his attention back to the woman and said, "How can I help you Ms.—?"

"Kravitz, Cheryl Kravitz. I'm here to take charge of this scene."

Timmy Jones showed no sign of backing down. He said, "This is our scene. We have it in hand. Thank you."

I was impressed with Timmy's spine. He was a good friend, but not someone you'd usually think of as standing up to the US government.

Agent Kravitz said, "I misspoke. I'm here to take charge of several of the people you have in custody. This is a matter of national security and I *do* have the authority." This was a woman who was used to getting what she wanted.

Timmy said, "Who do you want to take?"

Agent Kravitz leaned in the door and surveyed the room. Then she faced him again. "The three men in the kitchen and the injured woman for now." She looked back inside and added, "We'll decide how to handle the others after we take the ones in the kitchen."

"We're about to transport the woman to the hospital."

"We'll take care of any medical needs." The woman turned and signaled to a man in the closest SUV, who started to walk toward the cabin.

Timmy raised his hands, and I stepped closer to back him up. He said, "One of the men you want to take right now is suspected in a double homicide. The bald guy in the kitchen will be charged with assault. We can take care of both of those matters."

Agent Kravitz said, "Who did he assault?"

Now I spoke up. "Me." I reached up and touched my ear, which was still leaking a little blood.

"You call that an assault?"

"He did it with a KA-BAR knife. Maybe that's attempted murder."

She gave me a cold stare and said, "And you are . . . ?"

"Mitchum. I came for Bailey Mae."

The woman said, "Who's Bailey Mae?"

"The little girl your friends held in a cell up in that bunker. She's coming with me, and I don't care how many agents with guns try to stop me." I gave her the stink eye, although I think it had little impact.

Agent Kravitz looked at my ear and said, "So, Mr. Mitchum, you were trespassing when someone tried to stop you. Dress it up any way you want, but you got what you deserved."

"Dress it up any way you want, but this is bullshit. Those men in there had no due process. Your people ran amok."

"I never said they were 'my people.' I just said we were taking them. And that is exactly what is going to happen."

My blood was rising, and I felt the flash of heat in my face. "The other men have to stay. They need medical attention. There's no way we're gonna let you take those men with you." I had to look over at Timmy to make sure we were in agreement. I was going to need help if I took on the federal government in the form of Cheryl Kravitz.

Agent Kravitz considered my comments, then glanced back in the cabin at the men huddled in the living room. I could see her working through the scenarios in her head. All these witnesses could cause a lot of trouble. She couldn't take us. Could she?

Finally the federal agent said, "Be my guest, but the three men and the woman are coming with me right now."

"You don't care that one of the men is a murderer?"

"On the contrary, Mr. Mitchum, I do care and we will deal with that issue. But due to national security, that's not going to happen here in front of a bunch of locals like you."

Two of the men from the SUVs stepped past us into the cabin to gather up the people they intended to take. As long as Bailey Mae was safe and they didn't try to recapture any of these dispirited men, I didn't intend to engage in a shoot-out.

I stepped inside and herded Bailey Mae, Natty, and Hassan toward the group of men we had liberated. I stood between them and the Homeland Security agents as Agent Kravitz stepped inside and motioned for the former jailers to follow her.

No one said a word. At this point I didn't want Timmy and his people to risk getting hurt, either. Agent Kravitz paused by the door and took one last look around the cabin.

I glared at her.

The federal agent chose not to even acknowledge me and turned back to Timmy. "I'll need your people to get their vehicles out of the way so we can leave."

I stepped to the door and heard Agent Kravitz say to Timmy, "We will look into the need for filing any charges for assault on any of the men or women working here."

I couldn't help the snort that came out as I said, "Good luck with that." The truth was this woman did scare me a little bit. The whole situation was scary. No one would judge this as normal.

She looked at me and said, "I think you would do well to remain silent, Mr. Mitchum."

She used the phrase "remain silent" instead of "be quiet." She knew her shit, and she knew how to intimidate.

Watching the assholes I had tangled with walk freely toward the SUVs, I just couldn't keep my mouth shut. I leaned out the door, shaking off Natty and Bailey Mae, who tried to stop me. "This is bullshit! He's a murderer and people are not going to stand for it. We won't forget this."

Agent Kravitz didn't even turn around. She just called over her shoulder, "Neither will we."

When I turned, Bailey Mae darted into my arms. I squeezed her just to make sure it wasn't a dream. This was real. She was why I was here. But now I had other responsibilities.

Turning, I looked at the group of men we had rescued. I wasn't about to leave until I was certain they were safe. Timmy looked completely flummoxed but was starting to organize the stunned emergency workers again after everything had come to a halt when the feds showed up.

Three ambulances had pulled in. The injured woman had already been taken away by Homeland Security.

"Timmy," I said, "let's get three men into each ambulance and then a couple with each paramedic. We need to get them checked out."

"Yeah, good idea, Mitchum."

I didn't want to make it look like I was giving orders, but we had to get moving.

Hassan paused before he followed a paramedic out the door. He held out his hand, and when I took it, he said, "We will not forget this, my friend. What you did took great courage. Bailey Mae is lucky to have a cousin like you."

I gave him a smile and nod as I shook his hand.

Some of the others waved and shouted their thanks until it was just Timmy, Natty, Bailey Mae, and me.

"What do you think will happen to the people the feds took?"

Timmy shrugged. "I never saw anything like that. The sheriff told me they were legit and I had to let them take the prisoners. I hope they take action."

I slapped Timmy on the back as we walked toward our cars down at the front of the property. "You're a good man, Timmy." I thought he was naive, but his heart was in the right place and that was important to me.

I realized there was a big bad world out there and I'd spent most of my life in Marlboro, New York, trying to avoid it. The world worked in mysterious and unethical ways, but it was time I took my head out of the sand and stood up to it.

The one thing I wasn't going to let drop was Mabel's death. I knew in my heart it was connected to this mess, probably because she showed me photos of the three strangers. No matter what happened, I intended to find some answers, but that could wait for another day.

I wrapped my arm around Bailey Mae as we walked. I was thankful that at least I got what I had come for and couldn't wait to see Bailey Mae and her mother reunited. We had also managed to free the men held in those terrible conditions. Now, that was a victory I'd accept.

Life here in Marlboro had its moments.

ABOUT THE AUTHORS

JAMES PATTERSON has written more bestsellers and created more enduring fictional characters than any other novelist writing today. He lives in Florida with his family.

JAMES O. BORN is an award-winning crime and science-fiction novelist as well as a career law enforcement agent. A native Floridian, he still lives in the Sunshine State.

"ALEX CROSS, I'M COMING FOR YOU..."

Gary Soneji, the killer from *Along Came a Spider,* has been dead for more than ten years—but Cross swears he saw Soneji gun down his partner. Is Cross's worst enemy back from the grave?

Nothing will prepare you for the wicked truth.

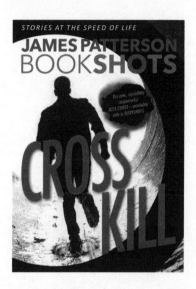

Read on for a special excerpt from the riveting Alex Cross story, available only from

BOOK**SHOTS**

A LATE WINTER STORM bore down on Washington, DC, that March morning, and more folks than usual were waiting in the cafeteria of St. Anthony of Padua Catholic School on Monroe Avenue in the northeast quadrant.

"If you need a jolt before you eat, coffee's in those urns over there," I called to the cafeteria line.

From behind a serving counter, my partner, John Sampson, said, "You want pancakes or eggs and sausage, you come see me first. Dry cereal, oatmeal, and toast at the end. Fruit, too."

It was early, a quarter to seven, and we'd already seen twenty-five people come through the kitchen, mostly moms and kids from the surrounding neighborhood. By my count, another forty were waiting in the hallway, with more coming in from outside, where the first flakes were falling.

It was all my ninety-something grandmother's idea. She'd hit the DC Lottery Powerball the year before and wanted to make sure the unfortunate received some of her good fortune. She'd partnered with the church to see the hot-breakfast program started.

"Are there any doughnuts?" asked a little boy, who put me in mind of my younger son, Ali.

He was holding on to his mother, a devastatingly thin woman with rheumy eyes and a habit of scratching at her neck.

"No doughnuts today," I said.

"What am I gonna eat?" he complained.

"Something that's good for you for once," his mom said. "Eggs, bacon, and toast. Not all that Cocoa Puffs sugar crap."

I nodded. Mom looked like she was high on something, but she did know her nutrition.

"This sucks," her son said. "I want a doughnut. I want two doughnuts!"

"Go on, there," his mom said, and pushed him toward Sampson.

"Kind of overkill for a church cafeteria," said the man who followed her. He was in his late twenties and dressed in baggy jeans, Timberland boots, and a big gray snorkel jacket.

I realized he was talking to me and looked at him, puzzled.

"Bulletproof vest?" he said.

"Oh," I said, and shrugged at the body armor beneath my shirt.

Sampson and I are major-case detectives with the Washington, DC, Metropolitan Police Department. Immediately after our shift in the soup kitchen, we were joining a team taking down a drug gang operating in the streets around St. Anthony's. Members of the gang had been known to take free breakfasts at the school from time to time, so we'd decided to armor up. Just in case.

I wasn't telling him that, though. I couldn't identify him as a known gangster, but he looked the part.

"I'm up for a PT test end of next week," I said. "Got to get used to the weight since I'll be running three miles with it on."

"That vest make you hotter or colder today?"

"Warmer. Always."

"I need one of them," he said, and shivered. "I'm from Miami, you know? I must have been crazy to want to come on up here."

"Why did you come up here?" I asked.

"School. I'm a freshman at Howard."

"You're not on the meal program?"

"Barely making my tuition."

I saw him in a whole new light then, and was about to say so when gunshots rang out and people began to scream.

DRAWING MY SERVICE PISTOL, I pushed against the fleeing crowd, hearing two more shots, and realizing they were coming from inside the kitchen behind Sampson. My partner had figured it out as well.

Sampson spun away from the eggs and bacon, drew his gun as I vaulted over the counter. We split and went to either side of the pair of swinging industrial kitchen doors. There were small portholes in both.

Ignoring the people still bolting from the cafeteria, I leaned forward and took a quick peek. Mixing bowls had spilled off the stainless-steel counters, throwing flour and eggs across the cement floor. Nothing moved, and I could detect no one inside.

Sampson took a longer look from the opposite angle. His face almost immediately screwed up.

"Two wounded," he hissed. "The cook, Theresa, and a nun I've never seen before."

"How bad?"

"There's blood all over Theresa's white apron. Looks like the nun's hit in the leg. She's sitting up against the stove with a big pool below her."

"Femoral?"

Sampson took another look and said, "It's a lot of blood."

"Cover me," I said. "I'm going in low to get them."

Sampson nodded. I squatted down and threw my shoulder into the door, which swung away. Half expecting some unseen gunman to open fire, I rolled inside. I slid through the slurry of two dozen eggs and came to a stop on the floor between two prep counters.

Sampson came in with his weapon high, searching for a target.

But no one shot. No one moved. And there was no sound except the labored breathing of the cook and the nun, who were to our left, on the other side of a counter, by a big industrial stove.

The nun's eyes were open and bewildered. The cook's head slumped but she was breathing.

I scrambled under the prep counter to the women and started tugging off my belt. The nun shrank from me when I reached for her.

"I'm a cop, Sister," I said. "My name is Alex Cross. I need to put a tourniquet on your leg or you could die."

She blinked, but then nodded.

"John?" I said, observing a serious gunshot wound to her lower thigh. A needle-thin jet of blood erupted with every heartbeat.

"Right here," Sampson said behind me. "Just seeing what's what."

"Call it in," I said, as I wrapped the belt around her upper thigh, cinching it tight. "We need two ambulances. Fast."

The blood stopped squirting. I could hear my partner making the radio call.

The nun's eyes fluttered and drifted toward shut.

"Sister," I said. "What happened? Who shot you?"

Her eyes blinked open. She gaped at me, disoriented for a moment, before her attention strayed past me. Her eyes widened, and the skin of her cheek went taut with terror.

I snatched up my gun and spun around, raising the pistol. I saw Sampson with his back to me, radio to his ear, gun lowered, and then a door at the back of the kitchen. It had swung open, revealing a large pantry.

A man crouched in a fighting stance in the pantry doorway.

In his crossed arms he held two nickel-plated pistols, one aimed at Sampson and the other at me.

With all the training I've been lucky enough to receive over the years, you'd think I would have done the instinctual thing for a veteran cop facing an armed assailant, that I would have registered *Man with gun!* in my brain, and I would have shot him immediately.

But for a split second I didn't listen to *Man with a gun!* because I was too stunned by the fact that I knew him, and that he was long, long dead.

IN THAT SAME INSTANT, he fired both pistols. Traveling less than thirty feet, the bullet hit me so hard it slammed me backward. My head cracked off the concrete and everything went just this side of midnight, like I was swirling and draining down a black pipe, before I heard a third shot and then a fourth.

Something crashed close to me, and I fought my way toward the sound, toward consciousness, seeing the blackness give way, disjointed and incomplete, like a jigsaw puzzle with missing pieces.

Five, maybe six seconds passed before I found more pieces and I knew who I was and what had happened. Two more seconds passed before I realized I'd taken the bullet square in the Kevlar that covered my chest. It felt like I'd taken a sledgehammer to my ribs and a swift kick to my head.

In the next instant, I grabbed my gun and looked for…

John Sampson sprawled on the floor by the sinks, his massive frame looking crumpled until he started twitching electrically, and I saw the head wound.

"No!" I shouted, becoming fully alert and stumbling over to his side.

Sampson's eyes were rolled up in his head and quivering. I grabbed the radio on the floor beyond him, hit the transmitter, and said, "This is Detective Alex Cross. Ten-Zero-Zero. Repeat. Officer down. Monroe Avenue and 12th Northeast. St. Anthony's Catholic School kitchen. Multiple shots fired. Ten-Fifty-Twos needed immediately. Repeat. Multiple ambulances needed, and a Life Flight for officer with head wound!"

"We have ambulances and patrols on their way, Detective," the dispatcher came back. "ETA twenty seconds. I'll call Life Flight. Do you have the shooter?"

"No, damn it. Make the Life Flight call."

The line went dead. I lowered the radio. Only then did I look back at the best friend I've ever had, the first kid I met after Nana Mama brought me up from South Carolina, the man I'd grown up with, the partner I'd relied on more times than I could count. The spasms subsided and Sampson's eyes glazed over and he gasped.

"John," I said, kneeling beside him and taking his hand. "Hold on now. Cavalry's coming."

He seemed not to hear, just stared vacantly past me toward the wall.

I started to cry. I couldn't stop. I shook from head to toe, and then I wanted to shoot the man who'd done this. I wanted to shoot him twenty times, completely destroy the creature that had risen from the dead.

Sirens closed in on the school from six directions. I wiped at my tears, and then squeezed Sampson's hand, before forcing myself to my feet and back out into the cafeteria, where the first patrol officers were charging in, followed by a pair of EMTs whose shoulders were flecked with melting snowflakes.

They got Sampson's head immobilized, then put him on a board and then a gurney. He was under blankets and moving in less than six minutes. It was snowing hard outside. They waited inside the front door to the school for the helicopter to come, and put IV lines into his wrists.

Sampson went into another convulsion. The parish priest, Father Fred Close, came and gave my partner the last rites.

But my man was still hanging on when the helicopter came. In a daze I followed them out into a driving snowstorm. We had to shield our eyes to duck under the blinding propeller wash and get Sampson aboard.

"We'll take it from here!" one EMT shouted at me.

"There's not a chance I'm leaving his side," I said, climbing in beside the pilot and pulling on the extra helmet. "Let's go."

The pilot waited until they had the rear doors shut and the gurney strapped down before throttling up the helicopter. We began to rise, and it was only then that I saw through the swirling snow that crowds were forming beyond the barricades set up in a perimeter around the school and church complex.

We pivoted in the air and flew back up over 12th Street, rising above the crowd. I looked down through the spiraling snow and saw everyone ducking their heads from the helicopter wash.

Everyone except for a single male face looking directly up at the Life Flight, not caring about the battering, stinging snow.

"That's him!" I said.

"Detective?" the pilot said, his voice crackling over the radio in my helmet.

I tugged down the microphone and said, "How do I talk to dispatch?"

The pilot leaned over and flipped a switch.

"This is Detective Alex Cross," I said. "Who's the supervising detective heading to St. Anthony's?"

"Your wife. Chief Stone."

"Patch me through to her."

Five seconds passed as we built speed and hurtled toward the hospital.

"Alex?" Bree said. "What's happened?"

"John's hit bad, Bree," I said. "I'm with him. Close off that school from four blocks in every direction. Order a door-to-door search. I just saw the shooter on 12th, a block west of the school."

"Description?"

"It's Gary Soneji, Bree," I said. "Get his picture off Google and send it to every cop in the area."

There was silence on the line before Bree said sympathetically, "Alex, are *you* okay? Gary Soneji's been dead for years."

"If he's dead, then I just saw a ghost."

WE WERE BUFFETED BY winds and faced near-whiteout conditions trying to land on the helipad atop George Washington Medical Center. In the end we put down in the parking lot by the ER entrance, where a team of nurses and doctors met us.

They hustled Sampson inside and got him attached to monitors while Dr. Christopher Kalhorn, a neurosurgeon, swabbed aside some of the blood and examined the head wounds.

The bullet had entered Sampson's skull at a shallow angle about two inches above the bridge of his nose. It had exited forward of his left temple. That second wound was about the size of a marble, but gaping and ragged, as if the bullet had been a hollow point that broke up and shattered going through bone.

"Let's get him intubated, on propofol, and into an ice bath and cooling helmet," Kalhorn said. "Take his temp down to ninety-two, get him into a CT scanner, and then the OR. I'll have a team waiting for him."

The ER doctors and nurses sprang into action. In short order, they had a breathing tube down Sampson's throat and were racing him away. Kalhorn turned to leave. I showed my badge and stopped him.

"That's my brother," I said. "What do I tell his wife?"

Dr. Kalhorn turned grim. "You tell her we'll do everything possible to save him. And you tell her to pray. You, too, Detective."

"What are his chances?"

"Pray," he said, then took off at a trot and disappeared.

I was left standing in an empty treatment slot in the ER, looking down at the dark blood that stained the gauze pads they'd used to clean Sampson's head.

"You can't stay in here, Detective," one of the nurses said sympathetically. "We need the space. Traffic accidents all over the city with this storm."

I nodded, turned, and wandered away, wondering where to go, what to do.

I went out in the ER waiting area and saw twenty people in the seats. They stared at my pistol, at the blood on my shirt, and at the black hole where Soneji's bullet had hit me. I didn't care what they thought. I didn't—

I heard the automatic doors *whoosh* open behind me.

A fearful voice cried out, "Alex?"

I swung around. Billie Sampson was standing there in pink hospital scrub pants and a down coat, shaking from head to toe from the cold and the threat of something far more bitter. "How bad is it?"

Billie's a surgical nurse, so there was no point in being vague. I described the wound. Her hand flew to her mouth at first, but then she shook her head. "It's bad. He's lucky to be alive."

I hugged her and said, "He's a strong man. But he's going to need your prayers. He's going to need all our prayers."

Billie's strength gave way. She began to moan and sob into my chest, and I held her tighter. When I raised my head, the people in the waiting room were looking on in concern.

"Let's get out of here," I muttered, and led Billie out into the hallway and to the chapel.

We went inside, and thankfully it was empty. I got Billie calmed down enough to tell her what had happened at the school and afterward.

"They've put him into a chemical coma and are supercooling his body."

"To reduce swelling and bleeding," she said, nodding.

"And the neurosurgeons here are the best. He's in their hands now."

"And God's," Billie said, staring at the cross on the wall in the chapel before pulling away from me to go down on her knees.

I joined her and we held hands and begged our Savior for mercy.

"I'M NOT ON TRIAL. SAN FRANCISCO IS."

Drug cartel boss the Kingfisher has a reputation for being violent and merciless. And after he's finally caught, he's set to stand trial for his vicious crimes—until he begins unleashing chaos and terror upon the lawyers, jurors, and police associated with the case. The city is paralyzed, and Detective Lindsay Boxer is caught in the eye of the storm.

Will the Women's Murder Club make it out alive—or will a courtroom shocker ensure their last breaths?

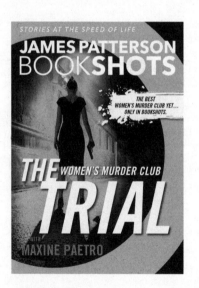

Read the shocking new Women's Murder Club story, available only from

BOOK**SHOTS**

WILL THE LAST HUMANS ON EARTH PLEASE TURN OUT THE LIGHTS?

As humans continue to be plagued by vicious animal attacks, zoologist Jackson Oz desperately tries to save the ones he loves—and the rest of mankind. But animals aren't the only threat anymore. Some humans are starting to evolve, too, turning into something feral and ferocious….

Could this savage new species save civilization—or end it?

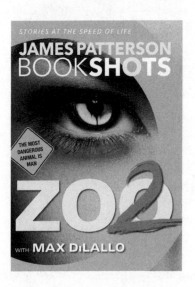

Read the high-adrenaline page-turner *Zoo 2*, available only from

BOOK**SHOTS**

SOME GAMES AREN'T FOR CHILDREN....

After a nasty divorce, Christy Moore finds her escape in Marty Hawking, who introduces her to all sorts of new experiences, including an explosive game called Make-Believe.

But what begins as innocent fun soon turns dark, and as Marty pushes the boundaries further and further, the game may just end up deadly.

Read the jaw-dropping thriller *Let's Play Make-Believe*, available only from

BOOKSHOTS

*Looking to Fall in Love in
Just One Night?*

Introducing BookShots Flames:

**original romances presented by James Patterson
that fit into your busy life**

Featuring Love Stories by

New York Times bestselling author Jen McLaughlin

New York Times bestselling author Samantha Towle

USA Today bestselling author Erin Knightley

Elizabeth Hayley

Jessica Linden

Codi Gary

Laurie Horowitz

…and many others!

Available only from

HER SECOND CHANCE AT LOVE MIGHT BE TOO GOOD TO BE TRUE....

When Chelsea O'Kane escapes to her family's inn in Maine, all she's got are fresh bruises, a gun in her lap, and a desire to start anew. That's when she runs into her old flame, Jeremy Holland. As he helps her fix up the inn, they rediscover what they once loved about each other.

Until it seems too good to last…

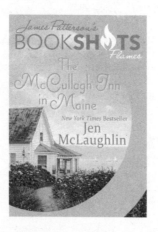

Read the stirring story of hope and redemption
The McCullagh Inn in Maine